"They came from another world," Jon recited confidently, "from far beyond the furthest star we can see. They came in vast ships and little ships that flew through the air. It was long ago when our ancestors were just savages. The first Starborn were wicked . . . then the good Starborn came and fought to set us free . . ."

Everyone on Rakath knows about the legendary Starborn. Few know of their amazing legacy. Through a chance encounter with a stranger, Jon becomes one of the few.

Soon the crippled beggar boy is involved in an adventure beyond his wildest imaginings.

QUEST

Dorothy Oxley

A LION PAPERBACK
Oxford · Batavia · Sydney

Copyright © 1990 Dorothy Oxley

Published by
Lion Publishing plc
Sandy Lane West, Oxford, England
ISBN 0 7459 1846 8
Lion Publishing Corporation
1705 Hubbard Avenue, Batavia, Illinois 60510, USA
ISBN 0 7459 1846 8
Albatross Books Pty Ltd
PO Box 320, Sutherland, NSW 2232, Australia
ISBN 0 7324 0170 4

British Library Cataloguing in Publication Data
Oxley, Dorothy
  Quest.
  I. Title
  823'.914 [J]

  ISBN 0-7459-1846-8

Library of Congress Cataloging in Publication Data
Oxley, Dorothy.
  Quest / Dorothy Oxley.
  p. cm. — (A Lion paperback)
  [1. Science fiction.] I. Title.
PZ7.09797Qu   1990
[Fic]—dc20

Printed and bound in Great Britain by
Cox and Wyman Ltd, Reading

CONTENTS

1

THE MEETING

"Go on, Wobblelegs! I dare you!"

Jon didn't bother to answer. He hadn't really been listening anyway. Ignoring Bok and Freth, he looked beyond the two boys and the crowded dock. It was a clear morning, so he could see right across to the northern shore. There beyond the wharf, beyond the market place, the roads climbed up to the very heart of the capital of Rakath — the Crystal City. And within the City was the Hall of Knights. Jon had never been there, but he loved to imagine it, and dream of the day when he would — just maybe — take his place there. It wasn't a dream he spoke about readily, because people tended to burst out laughing. But just for a moment he forgot everything else and imagined himself among the candidates, the boys who hoped to be trained as knights. Right now, they'd be out exercising in the courtyard. Wrestling, setting up their archery targets, and fighting with wooden swords . . .

"It'll be dead easy!" Bok hissed. "Look, there'll be all these country bumpkins crowded together on the ferry. If you stumble into them, they won't suspect anything, you being a cripple. But meanwhile, me and Freth will whip their purses."

Jon sighed. If only they'd go away and leave him to his daydreams!

"Tie rocks to your feet," he recommended wearily, "and go for a swim."

"You're scared," Bok jeered. "You've gone soft since you let the old brown crows and the Healers house and feed you. Do you wash behind your ears and say your prayers before you go to bed now, Staggerfoot?"

No, Jon decided. They obviously wouldn't go away unless he made them. Reluctantly, he reached for his crutches.

Bok had been trying to think up another interesting insult, but when Jon got up both he and his silent friend Freth took a step backwards. They knew all too well what Jon could do with those crutches. He could scuttle along surprisingly fast on his bent and twisted legs, while his strong arms and shoulders made the crutches lash out. And right now there was a nasty look in his eyes. Calling him names — but not too loudly — the two boys retreated, losing themselves in the gathering crowd.

Jon didn't pursue them far. He could see the ferry making its way across the water and realized he'd been wasting time. All these people waiting for the boat meant a chance to earn some money, and he couldn't afford to miss it.

Three years ago, he'd have waited by the ferry booth with his poor twisted legs on full display. Because he was small for his age and had a face much more innocent than the brain behind it, the women especially often took pity on him. But if it was a bad day for begging, he'd get up and stumble clumsily away through the crowds. The ones he stumbled against usually took a while to realize they'd lost something and, even when they did, few thought of the crippled beggar boy. Bok knew that — what he didn't know, or wouldn't accept, was that Jon was different now. Since he'd taken shelter with the Brown Brothers and Sisters, he'd given up both begging and stealing. And he wasn't going to start again. Brother Almar said crime grieved Yeveth, the Eternal One; Sister Zulie said it was like a poison hurting the thief as well as his victims. But most important of all, so far as Jon was concerned, Sir Kerouan didn't like it.

Thinking of Sir Kerouan, his hero, he smiled. It was such a radiant smile that a passing farmer's wife caught her breath, moved by the happy courage of this ragged boy with his pathetically twisted legs. Not enough good food, she thought sadly, for her own children were sturdy and straight. Next moment Jon found a ripe goldenfruit thrust into his hands, and a fresh bun. Then the woman, flushed slightly with embarrassment at her own good deed, was gone.

"Thank you, ma'am!" Jon called after her, biting eagerly into the bun and putting the fruit into his pocket. He was hungry, for he'd come out before breakfast, and he knew he had to eat more to build up his strength, so that one day the Healers could try to straighten his legs. Then maybe he could achieve his greatest dream and become a trainee knight himself.

Swinging his bag from his back, he sat down on the cobbles near the ferry booth and began to set out his tools. Two brushes, two clean rags, and a pot of colourless wax.

"Shine your boots, sirs and ladies?" he called

hopefully. Some of the farmers' boots were certainly dirty enough to need his services, but the men seemed more bothered about their vegetables and eggs than about looking smart. Also, farmers weren't famed for parting with money unless they had to. Young men and girls seeking a hiring, or out for a day's holiday, might prove better customers.

"You can't impress people if your boots are dirty!" Jon bellowed. "Let me help you look your best!"

But he'd waited too long. The ferry booth had opened and the crowd were jostling for tickets. After his brushes had been trodden on, and he'd been knocked over twice, Jon sighed and got out of the way. Maybe he'd do better with people coming off the ferry. Not that there'd be many, this early in the day.

"My boots could do with a clean, lad."

Jon looked at the boots first, then nodded. They were fine leather, but very muddy and dusty, and looked as if they'd travelled a good many miles. Their wearer was a slight, weary-looking man, with a friendly smile and warm grey eyes. He might have been a travelling minstrel, but he didn't have any kind of instrument strapped on his back, just an old knapsack. Still, he was a customer, and Jon set to work, first brushing off the encrusted dirt.

"You've come a long way, sir," Jon guessed as he brushed. "Are you a stranger to the city?"

If he was, he might want a guide. So far Jon had found little success in offering his services, even though he knew most of the southern side of the city like the back of his hand. People just didn't trust a crippled boy to go at their pace or stay the distance. But it was worth a try, and this man looked kind. From a very young age Jon had learned

10

to judge human beings, looking beneath their faces for something he could sense rather than see. It was a necessary ability, for there were people around with ugly, twisted desires, and a slum child could disappear without anyone asking too many awkward questions. But Jon knew instinctively that his grey-eyed customer was one of the good ones, the sort who give you money or food and speak to you as if you are human, not something that has crawled out from under a stone.

"If you need a guide, sir," he said hopefully, "I know the streets round here very well . . . "

The man smiled at him, but shook his head.

"Sorry, lad. I've got to go across to the Crystal City, and I know my way."

Jon shrugged away his disappointment and got on with polishing the man's boots. Out of the corner of his eye he could see Bok and Freth, trying to make themselves invisible in the thickest, noisiest part of the crowd while they waited for the ferry to dock. Perhaps they hadn't changed their plan to sneak aboard and rob its passengers.

"If you're taking the ferry, keep hold of your purse on board," Jon warned his customer. "There's pickpockets about."

"Thanks. I'll be careful," the man promised. Then, as Jon put the finishing touches to his boots, he reached into a pouch at his waist and drew out not one, but three copper coins.

"Here, lad. You've done a good job."

Jon stared at the coins. Every instinct told him to snatch them and say nothing, but a knight had to be beyond reproach. And one day — even if it sometimes seemed impossible — he was determined to be a knight.

"People usually only give me one," he said after a moment, feeling that the Brothers — and Sir Kerouan for that matter — would be proud of him. The man grinned.

"Take them," he insisted. "I've much to be thankful for, and I'm feeling generous. Why not spend one on a ferry ticket? You'll surely find customers in the market — or outside the park, since the ground will be muddy after the rains."

"Thanks, sir. I will!"

Jon beamed at the man, then added shyly: "If you're in the city long and want any odd jobs doing, sir, you can ask for me at the South Wharf Sanctuary. My name's Jon."

"And I'm Guyon. Well, good trading, Jon. I'm off to get my ticket."

Guyon. The name was faintly familiar, but Jon didn't know why, nor did he much care. Happily aware of the coins now in the secret inner pocket of his ragged shirt, he packed up his cleaning things and also joined the crowd which was now surging forward. He felt rich and important as he paid for his ticket and swung up the gargplank with all the confidence of someone who had a right to be there. Not like Bok and Freth! He was a tradesman. They were criminals. He felt very glad that he'd not agreed to join in their thieving plans, and not just because he could now feel pleasantly virtuous. They were crazy to think of picking pockets on the ferry. What if anyone caught them at it? Where could they run?

It was very crowded on the main deck and Jon saw that his customer, Guyon, had made his way to an upper deck where there were fewer people. Rather shyly, he joined the man there.

"I won't pester you, sir," he promised. "It's just too crowded down there."

The man smiled.

"You also get a better view here," he said. "And we'll be sailing any moment. See, they've loosed her fore and aft and now her sails are catching the wind."

It was the first time Jon had actually sailed, though he'd spent most of his life in the alleys around the docks and wharves. As the fat brown sails billowed and the ship lurched, he stumbled with the unexpected motion. But soon he recovered his balance, and looked in wonder at the receding wharf, the wide sweep of the bay, and the shore to which they were heading. Everything looked cleaner somehow, seen from a boat sweeping through the blue waters.

Below, people laughed as the movement of the boat threw them together. Everyone was in a good mood now because going to market was a special occasion. They either had money to spend, or hoped they soon would make some.

Jon wondered what Bok and Freth were doing. Once they'd been friends, and he'd tried to get them to come along to the home the Brown Brothers and Sisters ran for orphaned children. But the prospect of regular meals, albeit simple ones, was offset by the horrible fact that they were expected to wash, to work and even to learn to read and write. Jon hadn't liked the washing or the learning much at first either, but now he was used to it, and even enjoyed reading the few books the orphanage possessed. But neither Bok nor Freth had been willing to stay and give it a try.

He forgot them swiftly as Guyon touched his arm and pointed out across the water. Something gleamed oddly on the surface.

"Zid," the man said. "It's a stinging jellyfish. They sometimes come in on the tide — though normally, thank goodness, they stay out of the shallows. If you're ever in the water and you see one, get out fast."

"Can they kill you?"

"They can," the man confirmed, "and very painfully."

But the jellyfish was in the water, and they were on the ferry. Soon it was left tossing in their wake.

Jon leaned on the rail, gazing out across the bay. On the deck below, a small, dirty hand reached silently for a farmer's money-pouch . . .

"Hoy! Thief! Stop, thief!"

The yell made Guyon look down, and Jon went cold, old memories urging him to run until he remembered that he hadn't stolen anything for ages. Bok was trying to dodge through the crowd, away from a big and angry man. But everyone was reaching to grab him and, panicking, he blundered into the rail. Jon didn't see exactly what happened, but next moment Bok was screeching and falling, to hit the water with a splash; and several voices yelled together:

"Man overboard!"

"He can't swim!" Jon yelled, and started to scramble onto the rail. He at least could swim the full width of the Inner Dock — Sister Zulie had taught him, saying it was a good way to strengthen his legs. And although it looked a long way down to the water, he was poised to jump to the rescue when Guyon yanked him back.

"I'm stronger," the man said simply. "Look after

14

my backpack for me, and throw one of your crutches as near to the boy as you can."

Then he was gone, diving back towards Bok's struggling figure. Although the ferry captain had headed his craft into the wind as soon as he heard the warning cry, the barge was going too fast to stop at once, and the distance to Bok was widening. Jon used all the strength in his arms and shoulders to hurl a crutch, javelin-like, towards Bok but it still fell well short of him.

Guyon, however, had hit the water cleanly, surfaced, and was swimming with effortless strokes to the rescue, while two sailors had already begun to lower a rowing boat. Feeling half relieved, half cheated of a chance to be a hero, Jon knew there was nothing more that he could do except look after Guyon's bag. He picked it up and held it between himself and the rail as he leaned to watch the rescue.

Guyon had reached the crutch and was swimming with it. As he got near to Bok — who had already gone under once and come up screaming — he held the crutch out. Jon heard his voice clearly across the water:

"You're safe now. Grab this and I'll tow you to the boat."

Bok grabbed — in his blind panic he would have grabbed anything that might keep him alive. He seemed to be trying to drag himself up the crutch to grab Guyon as well, but the man used the wood to make him keep his distance. All the time he was talking to Bok, commanding but gentle, and swimming back towards the barge with the boy in tow.

By now the ferry had stopped, and the rowing boat splashed into the water. But a new danger was coming. Jon saw it first — another odd, shining

15

patch behind a wavecrest, bearing down on the man and the boy. Only minutes before he wouldn't have known what it was, but now he shouted a warning.

"Zid, sir! Behind you!"

Grabbing his other crutch, he hurled it towards the shiny patch. Afterwards he would wonder how he'd managed to throw it so far. As it was it missed the zid but fell close to Guyon. The man grabbed it with his free hand. Now he could only kick with his legs, and Bok, whimpering in terror, was no help at all. But Guyon had seen the zid and, trying to get them both out of its way, he held the crutch out as a barrier. The sailors in the boat had also seen it, and sent their craft skimming across the last few yards of water.

Zulie had tried to teach Jon to pray to Yeveth, the loving creator of all things, when he was afraid or troubled, or even full of joy. He tried to pray now, but it still seemed strange talking silently in his head to an all-powerful being he couldn't see.

"Yeveth, save them from the jellyfish — help them, please . . . "

A scream rent the air, followed by a frantic splashing. At first Jon thought the zid had stung someone, but it was just Bok. He'd seen the jellyfish, let go of the crutch, and was beating the water in his frantic attempts to get away. He was almost swimming — but not quite. However, the boat was now close enough for one of the sailors to hook him with a long boathook and haul him in. Bok grabbed the boat and might have capsized it, but the sailor neatly knocked him out before dragging him on board. Meanwhile, to Jon's intense relief, Guyon also scrambled into the safety of the boat.

Someone on the lower deck started a cheer and

soon most of the crowd were joining in. Jon was so relieved that he failed to notice his crutches still floating forlornly in the water. But the sailor with the boathook fished them in before both men rowed back to the ferry. Soon the boat and its occupants were being hauled aboard.

Jon could walk without his crutches, but clumsily, and he didn't want to try it on a swaying deck. So he didn't attempt to go down to the lower deck, to wriggle through the crowd and greet Guyon. He waited while the man disappeared in a swarm of people who wanted to congratulate him, waited patiently as the ferry got under way again and all the excitement died down. As he waited, he listened with interest to the voices drifting up to him.

"A brave man!"

"You know who he is, don't you? It's Guyon of Castelmar."

"The penitent?"

"None other."

Penitent? It meant 'one who is sorry' — but sorry for what? Surely he couldn't be a thief? Seized by sudden, inexplicable curiosity, Jon opened the man's bag and glanced inside. But it held no loot. Just a change of clothes on top of some funny looking roots and a muddy metal thing which might be a shield boss or a bowl, not nearly as interesting as the old soldier's helmet stuck down one side of the pack. That seemed to suggest that Guyon might be, or have been, a warrior, even though he carried no weapons. Still, it was none of his business and Jon felt a bit ashamed of his curiosity as he closed the rucksack again. After all, Guyon had trusted him with it.

The man reappeared a few minutes later, wearing what looked like some seaman's spare clothes, and carrying Jon's crutches. He smiled, but his face looked pale and drawn.

"You saved us both with your warning and that crutch," he said softly. "Luckily, the zid was a small one, with short stingers. But the tail end of one caught my arm."

Raising his sleeve, he showed an angry scarlet weal, throbbing on swollen flesh. Jon gasped.

"I haven't told anyone else, because I don't want a fuss," the man explained. "But it's painful and I'd welcome some salve. Do you know of a Healer near where we dock?"

"Sister Zulie has a clinic in the market, every market day!" Jon said eagerly. "I'll take you to her. Here's your rucksack, sir."

Guyon's whispered "Thank you" sounded almost like a prayer. For a moment, an expression Jon couldn't quite read flickered in the man's eyes as he opened the rucksack and looked inside. But then he reached in and drew out a pair of trousers, producing a small knife from the pocket before he put them back and swung the rucksack casually onto his shoulders. Jon glanced curiously at the knife, and tried not to let his envy show. It wasn't a weapon, but it was the best penknife he'd ever seen, with a bone handle and two sharp folding blades. With a knife like that you could carve sticks, maybe even shape a bow and arrows if you knew how. And the longer blade would come in very handy for gutting fish.

"For you," Guyon said quietly, holding it out. "A very small thank-you."

"For me? But . . . "

Jon stared in delight and disbelief from the knife to the man. Then, seeing Guyon meant it, he put the knife in his own pocket. In that moment he promoted Guyon to his number two hero, after the Knight Champion, Sir Kerouan.

Shouts and a heavy thumping sound announced that the ferry had docked and the gangplank was down. Holding his hurt arm, Guyon got to his feet. Jon thought the man looked even paler now, beneath his tan. Concerned, he scanned the bustling quay and the market beyond until he saw what he was looking for — a patched brown tent with a red and white flag flying.

"There's Zulie's clinic," Jon said eagerly. "She's the best Healer in Rakath. She'll help you."

Guyon nodded.

"I'll be glad of her services," he admitted. "My arm feels as if it's on fire."

Guyon shuddered briefly, and Jon guessed that he was thinking about the agonizing death that could so easily have been his.

"Come," the boy said firmly. "Lean on me if you feel faint. When I've got my crutches, I'm much stronger than I look."

The questions echoing in his head as to who and what Guyon really was would have to wait. The important thing was to ease the man's pain.

Confident and determined, Jon led his new-found friend to Sister Zulie's tent of healing.

2

A DANGEROUS GIFT

There were six patients in the tent when Jon parted the flap with his crutch and led Guyon in. Five sat waiting; the sixth, a child, lay peacefully asleep while a young woman in the brown robes of a Healer dressed his scalded hand and arm. Her slender hands were skilled and beautiful; maybe her face, too, had been lovely once. But now she was pitifully disfigured by the disease called lucar, and though her eyes were alive with kindness, she could not see. Jon was so used to Zulie that he rarely noticed her disfigurement or her blindness, but Guyon looked at her with shock and pity that quickly turned to admiration for her obvious ability. This Healer knew what she was doing, and he urgently needed her help. The pain was sending shock waves through his body, making him feel faint, and he almost collapsed on the bench at the end of the queue. Jon went across to the Healer.

"Could you see my friend next, Sister Zulie?" he begged. "He's been stung by a zid and he's in a lot of pain."

"A zid?" Alarm in her voice, the woman stopped what she was doing.

"Take me to him now!" she ordered. "How badly has he been stung, Jon? How old, how fit is he?"

Guyon spoke swiftly, to calm her natural fear. He knew that, in a child, even a small sting sometimes proved fatal.

"It's all right, Sister," he said. "I'm a grown man, and tough as old boots. It's just a small welt on my arm. Some salve to ease the pain is all I need. I can wait my turn."

The Healer smiled, relaxing a little; but she had learned to scan the full range of pain, fear and weakness in her patients' voices. This man was unafraid, but he was suffering a great deal.

"No," she said quietly. "You can't wait. Jon, go to my bag and bring me the small, rough brown pot of salve. Now, sir, if you'd give me your injured arm . . . "

She knelt in front of Guyon and he put his arm into her waiting hands. Even as she touched him, his pain seemed to ease slightly and his eyes widened. He'd heard of Healers who were so close to Yeveth, so full of compassion, that their very touch could cure. But this young woman seemed more practical than mystical. Allowing her fingers to see for her, she traced the sting and the swelling around it, then felt his pulse. Meanwhile, Jon came hurrying over with the pot of salve. It was white and smelt of many things, including the sap of a rare herb called aras, very precious to Healers. It was effective too. The Healer had barely rubbed it into Guyon's sting when the flames of agony dulled to embers of pain. Severe enough still, but bearable now.

Guyon had got to the stage of clenching his teeth; now he relaxed.

"Thank you, Healer," he breathed. "That's a lot better. Now I mustn't hold up your clinic any longer. Let me pay you, and I'll be on my way."

The woman smiled, and her smile caught at Guyon's heart, for it whispered of the beauty that must once have been hers before disease took its toll.

"You will not be on your way," she said gently, but with clear command. "Your body has been shocked, and your heart is racing. If you don't lie down for a while your body will take matters into its own hands, and you'll faint."

"My body," Guyon answered, half amused and half determined, "will do what it's told by my mind!"

The blind woman raised her eyebrows.

"I have heard the same from knights and athletes who insist on pushing themselves beyond sensible limits," she argued. "In the end, their bodies and minds pay a cruel price. Will the world stop, sir, because you rest for an hour? If you have an appointment to keep, I'm sure Jon here will take a message for you."

"Gladly!"

One of the other patients, a wiry old man with a boil on his neck, joined the debate.

"Best do as she says, lad," he said. "Sister Zulie knows what she's talking about."

Guyon, well aware of his heart's rapid beat and a certain light-headedness, couldn't deny that they were right. But he had one last argument.

"I need to see Sir Kerouan," he explained quietly. "It's only a mile or so from here to the Hall of Knights. I'll be fine."

"But Sir Kerouan is here in the market place!"

the Healer exclaimed in delighted triumph. "He makes himself available, once each month, to hear anybody's grievances against the Order of Knights. Jon will run across and ask him to come and see you. Now you just lie down on that straw mattress in the corner of the tent and rest."

Despite himself, Guyon laughed.

"Oh, Healer!" he protested. "I'd hate to come against you in serious debate! But you win — I'll do as I'm told. Jon, could you just tell Sir Kerouan that Guyon of Castelmar is here, with something for him?"

"Right! Where is he, Sister Zulie?"

Jon's eyes were shining. What a day! Three copper coins, a ferry ride, an adventure, the knife — and now he'd be able actually to talk to his hero, the Knight Champion of Rakath. He was out of the tent the second he knew where to go, swinging through the crowd with practised ease. Normally he would have paused to stare at the acrobats and conjurors who entertained the crowds, but he could see them on another day. To see Sir Kerouan was special.

His mind went back to the day when they had first met, a cruel winter's day. Through long freezing hours Jon had sat in a doorway, begging, only to gain a few coins and some stale bread rolls. Then even these had been stolen from him by a gang of older boys, who had left him bruised and bleeding in the snow. Many people had gone by, ignoring him as he dragged himself miserably away — for in those days his legs had been very weak and he'd had no crutches. But then Sir Kerouan had come along, and picked him up, and carried him to Sister Zulie for healing. It was thanks to Sir Kerouan that the doors to a whole new life had opened up for

Jon; a life where, for the first time, he knew love and kindness, and hope.

Sir Kerouan was special.

There was a small law office in the market, where public scribes would draw up contracts for sale of goods or hire of services. It was here that Jon found Sir Kerouan, relaxing with the scribe who was on duty. Out of armour, he still looked like a knight — tall and strong, his muscles swelling beneath the black velvet of his skin. His face was strong, too, but with lines of laughter rather than cruelty, and lips that fell naturally into a smile. The smile widened when he saw Jon.

"Hello, my friend!" Sir Kerouan greeted him cheerfully. "What brings you here? Not a grievance, I hope?"

Jon took a moment to find his voice, then quickly blurted out his message. At once the knight rose.

"A zid sting?" he asked. "How did that happen?"

Jon told him, and the man nodded, his smile warm and gentle now.

"Guyon never has lacked courage," Kerouan murmured. "Well, we need not keep him waiting. My time here is almost over."

"I don't think anyone will come now," the scribe agreed. "If they do, I'll take the details for you, sir."

"Thanks, Pek. Right, Jon. Let's go!"

Proudly, Jon swung out ahead of Sir Kerouan, to lead the way. He looked a bit like a small, tattered tug preceding a majestic warship, but he felt magnificently important. Sir Kerouan remembered his name and called him friend! So what if people glanced at him with amusement or pity in their faces. So what, even, that his legs were twisted. To the Knight Champion of Rakath, he was someone.

So, it appeared, was Guyon. For Sir Kerouan went straight to the mattress where the man lay, and knelt beside it. Guyon sat up with a grin that was strangely shy.

"I meant to come to you, Sir Kerouan," he murmured. "Not to bring you running. But I've been bullied into obedience by the good Healer here."

The young woman, now lancing the old man's boil, heard and chuckled. Sir Kerouan laughed also.

"Sister Zulie has a way of winning obedience," he agreed. "But — welcome back, Guyon."

"You really mean it."

Suddenly grave, Kerouan nodded. For a moment neither man spoke and Jon watched them curiously. They seemed to share a secret which neither of them wanted to talk about. He wondered what it was. Then Guyon reached for his rucksack.

"The aras roots," he said, "and — a small gift in thanks for your past kindness. Something I found in the wastelands which will do better in your hands than in mine. But I'd ask you to take it to the Hall of Knights and not look inside till you are safely there."

There was something in his eyes, in his voice, which seemed half way between anguish and laughter. Sir Kerouan stared at him, puzzled, and then shrugged.

"As you wish, Guyon. I know I can trust you."

Guyon grinned.

"You mean that too!" he said. "Though many people would disagree with you. And, Sir Kerouan — would you humour me by taking my bag to the Hall at once? And now my quest is over, perhaps . . . ?"

"I shall ask permission for you to have a long time

of rest, as my guest," Kerouan said at once. Swinging the rucksack onto his back, he looked at Guyon once more, affectionately.

"I'll be back for you," he promised. Then he smiled at Jon.

"How'd you like to see the Hall of Knights?"

Like? Jon almost pinched himself to make sure he wasn't dreaming.

"Oh, yes, sir!" he whispered.

"Come, then."

Too happy even for words, Jon followed his hero out of the tent, through the market and up the tree-lined street which climbed towards the Crystal City. As they moved upwards, the streets became wider, the shops and houses bigger and more gracious. The Crystal City, heart of the capital, was the Old City, where windows of pure crystal split the morning sunlight into rainbows. Here the buildings were of stone, mellowed by time to purest cream.

The Hall of Knights itself lay behind a green area where the young trainee knights, the Athali, and the candidates often practised. Once, no poor person would have dared approach its gates, but now the two guards showed no surprise when Kerouan entered with a ragged boy in tow.

Once inside, they passed down a corridor hung with shields and trophies. Jon's eyes grew wide as saucers, and Kerouan explained that every knight still alive had his ceremonial shield here. The miniature versions higher on the wall — hundreds of them — belonged to past knights, now dead. Six shields hung together, edged with beaten gold. These had belonged to the greatest men in history — the Knight Heroes, each of whom had been instrumental in saving the Empire of Rakath from some terrible disaster.

"There's one shield here turned around," Jon said as they walked along. "Shall I turn it right way up, sir?"

But Kerouan's face grew sad, and he shook his head.

"No, Jon. That belongs to a dishonoured knight, so it's meant to be like that."

"Who was he? What did he do?"

"His name was Sir Valthor. You'd have been only a baby when it happened. He was a Knight Defender, the youngest ever to gain that rank, and everyone thought well of him. But he tried to steal the Helmets."

Jon looked puzzled. "What Helmets?" he asked.

Kerouan didn't answer for a moment. Then he said quietly: "The Helmets of Knowledge. We don't talk about them much. What do you know about the Starborn, Jon?"

The boy grinned. He'd never learned history, but he knew by heart nearly all the ballads that minstrels sang in the wharfside inns.

"They came from another world," he recited confidently, "from far beyond the furthest star we can see. They came in vast ships and little ships that flew through the air. It was long ago when our ancestors were just savages. The first Starborn were wicked. They enslaved our ancestors, did horrible things to some of them, and took all they wanted from our world. Then the good Starborn came and fought to set us free. All of them had terrible weapons that could destroy a city in minutes, or spread poisonous death for miles. But the good Starborn won."

Sir Kerouan smiled approval.

27

"Yes," he confirmed. "They won. They set us free, and taught us many things — especially our true faith, the Way of Yeveth. There were other things they could have taught us, but our ancestors weren't ready to learn them. So they left behind Helmets of Knowledge. If you put one on your head it imprints its knowledge onto your memory. We don't know how it works, but when you wear a helmet, suddenly all the Starborn knowledge it holds becomes yours."

Thinking of the struggle he'd had with some of his own lessons, Jon smiled wistfully. These Helmets sounded a much easier way of learning.

"But why did this Valthor want to steal them?" he asked. "Couldn't he have asked to wear them?"

Sir Kerouan shook his head.

"No. You see, our wisest men have always feared that if we knew all the Starborn knowledge we might use it for evil, as some of them did. They hid many of the Helmets, and kept only two kinds. The ones that taught helpful, harmless things like basic healing, farming and craft skills — these the Guildmasters were allowed to use. But the ones that taught how to make some of the Starborn machines, which might be used for war — these were guarded and nobody, not even the Emperor, was allowed to wear them."

Sir Kerouan sighed, glancing again at the reversed shield.

"But Valthor," he explained, "thought this was weak and foolish. He wanted the Empire of Rakath to rule the world and maybe even the stars. Nobody dreamed what he was planning except his friend, Sir Guyon. Guyon was a rebellious young man then, who wanted to change the world. He thought the forbidden Helmets might hold useful knowledge. He wanted to wear them and find out."

"Guyon?" Jon breathed, but Kerouan was still telling his story so he didn't interrupt.

"Together, they managed to get into the chamber where the Helmets were kept. Valthor was born with the power of mind-link, as happens sometimes in our people. It seems to run in families, and many of the best Healers have it."

Jon nodded, understanding. Sister Zulie had this ability to link her mind directly with someone else's. She used it when soothing speech wasn't enough to calm a hurt and frightened patient. By touching their mind, she could gently unravel the knots of pain and fear, and help them into the 'healing sleep'. It wasn't magic, just a natural ability which some people had.

"Usually, when mind-link powers are discovered in a child," Kerouan continued, "the Priests teach them how to seek Yeveth's help to use their abilities for good purposes. But Valthor had kept his a secret, and that night he used it to hypnotize the guards. However, an old priest was there, a man so close to Yeveth that no evil power could touch his mind. Valthor wanted to kill him, but Guyon wasn't the sort to permit the murder of an unarmed old man. So they fought. And by the time Guyon fell wounded, the alarm had been raised."

Sir Kerouan paused. It was almost as if it hurt him to recall that shameful night. Then he continued his story. "The Helmets were kept safe, but Valthor escaped, killing several people in the process. Now he's an outlaw, and he's gathered a cult of dangerous rebels about him — people prepared to use their mental powers for evil ends. They call themselves the Magos. So now you know why he is dishonoured and his shield turned round."

"I see," Jon agreed, faintly shocked. He'd known plenty of villains in his young life, but somehow it had never occurred to him that even knights could turn bad.

"And . . . Sir Guyon? Is he the Guyon I met?" he asked.

"Yes," Sir Kerouan confirmed, and led Jon over to another shield. This one was the right way round but had a thick bar across it. On the bar were seven silver stars.

"This is Guyon's shield," the knight explained. "After he'd recovered from his wound, he stood trial and pleaded guilty. He was sentenced to death but the Emperor granted his plea to die by the way of penitence. That means he has to undertake quests which will benefit the people of Rakath but are deadly dangerous. Most men die on their first, or at best their second, quest. These seven stars honour Guyon's seven successful quests — and now he's returned from another. He's fast becoming a legend!"

Now Jon knew why the man's name had seemed so familiar. He'd heard ballads sung in many inns about Guyon of Castelmar.

"The last quest was to gather aras roots," Kerouan said. "Sister Zulie may have told you how vital this herb is to Healers, but all the plants in our Empire were killed by blight. Guyon went to find more — in the heart of enemy territory. And he had to pass through the Wastelands to get there."

Kerouan glanced at the bag he held, then changed direction abruptly.

"The Emperor himself is here today, in conference

with Sir Lorak, our Grand Master," he explained. "Let's take what Guyon brought directly to them. It's Emperor Kolris who must officially record his quest as completed — and grant him, hopefully, a long rest before the next. He deserves that, at least."

Jon stared at the Knight, painfully conscious of his ragged clothes.

"I can't go with you to the Emperor!" he protested. "I'll make my way back to Zulie now. I mean, this is none of my business. It was great of you to show me the Hall of Knights, but . . . "

He ran out of words and stood, flushed and awkward, wanting to turn tail and run. Sir Kerouan rested one hand on his shoulder.

"You are as much his subject as I, and Kolris wants to get better acquainted with his ordinary subjects," he said. "Also, I want you to tell how Guyon saved that boy's life today. It could count in his favour and earn him a longer reprieve."

Reprieve. Jon shuddered, suddenly understanding what it really meant to be sentenced to the way of penitence. It wasn't just a bright adventure. In fact, it was almost more cruel than having your head chopped off. Then you only had to screw up your courage to face death once, and it was all over. Guyon, that kind man with laughing grey eyes, had already been sent to face death eight times, and he'd soon have to do so again. Swallowing hard, Jon nodded. He was willing to see the Emperor if there was a chance it might help Guyon.

"All right, sir," he agreed.

But he was trembling slightly when Sir Kerouan explained their business to a guard who stood outside one of the rooms. The man, a huge Thassan, listened in silence and then let them in. At the far

31

end of the room two men, one middle aged and one young, were poring over a map on a table. As the knight and the boy entered, they looked up. Sir Lorak was a Northern Islander, a tall, broad man with a fierce reddish beard and a scar across his face which gave him a permanent mocking smile. His eyes were a bright, intelligent blue. The young Emperor, Kolris, looked quite frail beside him, but Jon knew the man had won the rank of Knight Questor before taking the throne. Kolris was strikingly handsome in the typical copper-skinned, dark-haired way of his royal house, and he smiled at both his visitors.

Sir Kerouan bowed low. Jon tried, but it was almost impossible with crutches.

"Sire. My Lord," Sir Kerouan began respectfully. "Guyon has completed his quest and I bring the aras he has gathered. The man himself is lying in a Healer's tent in the market place — he was stung by a zid. I brought Jon here to tell you how it happened."

Jon was not normally lost for words. But in the company of two such great men he stumbled a little. What could they know of boys like Bok who stole for a living — and how much should he tell of his own small part in the drama? In the end he kept it simple, and blurted out his story in about two minutes. The Grand Master's mocking smile was belied by the kindness in his eyes as he listened, and read between the lines. Seeing the boy's twisted legs, he felt almost ashamed. They were, he guessed, a legacy of malnourishment, of the bad old days of which he'd also been a part. As a young knight he'd been far too wrapped up in adventures and martial campaigns ever to think of the needs of poor people in his own country. Now he was Grand Master of a changed Order slowly groping its way towards a different kind of honour, where justice and service mattered more than rituals and glory. He looked fondly at Kerouan, who was living proof of all that was good in the new ways. Yet in a sense it was Guyon who had forced them to think of change.

"Thank you, Jon," Lorak said gently as the boy finished. "Now, Sir Kerouan, let's see what Guyon has brought us."

The Knight opened Guyon's rucksack, removing the man's spare clothes and old helmet before tipping out the aras roots. Jon counted fourteen odd-looking brown, twisted things with only tiny pink buds to show where new shoots would grow once they were planted. Kolris picked one up, handling it reverently.

"These will help to save many lives," he murmured. "Guyon has done well."

"I'll have these taken to the College of Healers at once, Sire," Lorak promised. "Is this all of them?"

Sir Kerouan reached into the bag to make sure, and drew out the mud-covered, curved metal object which Jon had glimpsed on the ferry. Puzzled, he began to brush the mud away with his hand.

"Guyon spoke of a gift, something he found which he thought would be of more use to me than to him," he said. "I suppose this is it."

The mud had hardened and suddenly a great piece of it fell away, to reveal the thing more clearly. It was very light and seemed to be carved with runic signs — raised squiggles and lines of metal. The inside was padded with some kind of material, so it wasn't a bowl. Jon, trying to guess what it was, took a moment to realize that Sir Kerouan had become very still and silent, like an ebony statue, while the Emperor was staring at the thing in wide-eyed disbelief. Lorak, too, had taken a step forward, his whole body as tense as a drawn bowstring.

"It can't be!" he whispered.

Kerouan smiled, his eyes radiant.

"Yet it must be," he answered simply. "What else looks like this? It has to be a knowledge Helmet of the Starborn. Yeveth alone knows where he found it — but he brought it back to us! What that must have cost . . . "

Still totally bewildered, Jon stood silently, knowing they had all forgotten that he was even there. So this was one of the Helmets Sir Kerouan had told him about! Perhaps one of those the wise men of centuries ago had hidden. It didn't look very special. Yet Sir Valthor's shield was the wrong way round because he'd tried to steal helmets just like this.

"And I carried it!" Jon thought in pride and wonder. "I looked after it for Guyon!"

"Do you think he wore it himself?" the Emperor asked softly. Kerouan's smile deepened.

"I have no doubt he did," he murmured. "Yet he still brought it back to us. Sire, I must go at once and thank him!"

"Without even hearing what the Helmet has to tell us?" Sir Lorak asked, surprised. "It could be knowledge that will help us all — or something so dangerous we must guard it forever."

"A few more moments won't matter," Kolris argued reasonably. "Sir Kerouan — put on the Helmet, please. You have the right. I don't doubt that it was your kindness to Guyon which made him decide to bring it back to us."

Kerouan seemed about to protest; then, yielding, he fitted the silver skull-cap on his head. Nothing happened, as far as Jon could see, except that the Knight Champion suddenly seemed to be looking at something distant and wonderful, hearing something too, while Jon heard only his own breathing and the calls of birds in the trees outside. The boy began to fidget slightly, for his legs had carried him a fair distance and they were starting to ache. But he didn't fidget much because Kerouan was at his side — and in another world, perhaps.

Then, abruptly, it was over. Sir Kerouan took off the Helmet and handed it back to the young Emperor.

"It gives the location of a ship in which some of the Starborn came," he said after a moment. His voice was calm but his eyes still held visions. "It tells why they came, and that they left their ship and its knowledge for those who would one day be wise enough to understand how to use it for good."

Neither Lorak nor the Emperor spoke immediately. Both looked stunned. Then Kolris said, almost in a whisper, "Yes, Sir Kerouan. Go to Guyon. Give him my humble thanks, too, and tell him that if there is a way to revoke his sentence, it will be done. Meanwhile, he will be treated as an honoured knight."

"Then come back here at once," Lorak commanded. "We'll need to call in those who have a right to share the Helmet's knowledge — and of course it will need to be transferred to the Inner Temple and carefully guarded. Also, as Knight Champion, you'll need to organize and lead an immediate expedition to find this ship."

Kerouan's eyes blazed with eager delight.

"Gladly, Sir!"

"Now — as to Guyon and this lad . . . "

Finding himself suddenly the centre of attention, Jon flushed and looked appealingly at Sir Kerouan. He could guess the problem.

"I won't breathe a word to anyone until you say I can," he promised, though it was going to be very, very hard.

"But you still may be in danger," Sir Lorak said. "There are enemies who would do anything to gain a prize like a Starborn ship. Even friends could be tempted! And you say you held the bag while Guyon rescued that boy. If anyone so much as thinks you might have worn the Helmet and learned the location of the ship . . . "

The Knight didn't go into details, but Jon read the warning in his eyes. Kidnap, torture . . . He gulped as Sir Lorak continued, "Kerouan, I think you'd best take the boy with you, collect Guyon, and escort them both to the safety of the Western Keep. Better still, take young Zak with you and let him take over as soon as you've spoken to Guyon. Zak is utterly trustworthy and I want you back as soon as possible."

"I'll use a chariot."

So it was that Jon found himself following Sir Kerouan to the stables, where the young knight Zak had already harnessed two silvery haas to a light chariot. It was designed for travel, not for battle, and with Kerouan's sure hands on the reins they sped back down towards the market place, slowing all too soon as the crowd began to thicken. The ride took only minutes and Jon sighed when it was over, for he'd longed to try his hands at the reins. It would be so wonderful to control the power and beauty of the haas. How splendid they were, muscles flowing beneath their leathery coats, their sturdy clawed legs bending slightly as they came to a stop outside Zulie's tent and relaxed. In a chariot, his handicap wouldn't matter, Jon thought. The haas would be his legs and they could outrun the wind.

Sir Zak hadn't said a word on the short journey but, as he helped Jon down, he winked and whispered, "I'll give you a lesson at the reins when we go to the Keep. As soon as we've picked up Guyon . . ."

But neither Guyon nor Zulie was there — only a flustered-looking girl in the pale blue of an apprentice Healer. Jon recognized Mirita, from the South Wharf Sanctuary.

"There's been a bad accident at the wharf," she blurted. "A seaman fell between his ship and the dock wall and was crushed. Brother Almar is able to operate, but he needed Sister Zulie to send the man into the Healing Sleep — only she has the skill. So I came to fetch her and she's gone back."

"What about the patient who was here, Guyon?"

"The man stung by a zid? He insisted he was well enough to take her back. I'd sailed over in the Sanctuary boat, you see, because the ferry had gone; and Zulie said I must stay here and try to help any patients who came."

Kerouan smiled wryly, for he thought he could guess Guyon's motives. In giving up the Helmet he'd given up all his ambitions, his dreams of glory. More than words ever could, the action spoke of just how much the Castelmaran had changed. Sir Kerouan felt sure that Yeveth the Eternal was gently drawing the man's soul into his net, winning his heart and mind. Yet Guyon was proud, and unwilling to admit the change in himself. He must have been glad when the emergency summons came to Zulie and gave him a chance to vanish, a little time to gather his emotional defences.

But it gave Kerouan a problem.

"Go to the South Wharf Sanctuary," he ordered Sir Zak. "But forget the Keep. Just stay with Jon and Guyon in the Sanctuary itself. They may well be safer there anyway. Anyone trying to attack the Sanctuary would risk being lynched by half the local people!"

Zak grinned and nodded.

"I'll have to return," the Knight Champion continued. "I'll just write a note for you to take to Guyon."

A pad lay on Zulie's table. As Sir Kerouan tore off a sheet and wrote swiftly, Sir Zak moved over and glanced at other sheets already pinned on a spike. Healers usually made a brief note of every patient or visit to their clinics and Zulie, despite her blindness, was no exception. Her neat writing followed faint lines scratched across each page. The last page was in a different hand — Mirita's? Zak read her words with interest.

"So," he murmured, "a White Sister came asking after the man stung by a zid?"

Mirita nodded.

"Yes, Sir. Not long after Sister Zulie had gone. But I was stitching up a child's cut hand and the poor thing was screaming and crying — even though I'd made sure it wouldn't hurt. I was a bit flustered and didn't pay the Sister much attention, I'm afraid. I just told her he was much better and that he'd gone."

Zak glanced at Kerouan, a question in his eyes, but the Knight Champion did not look troubled. The White Sisters were devout and gifted scholars and craftswomen. Even the Emperor's older sister, Princess Halina, had joined their ranks.

"A White Sister?" he said. "No doubt she'd heard some exaggerated market rumour and was concerned. I don't think we need fear any evil in that direction!"

Later, Jon would remember those words. And know that Sir Kerouan had been terribly, tragically mistaken.

3

TREACHERY

"Yes, sister?"

A White Abbess was supposed to have no favour-
ites. But Mother Sarana could not help feeling a
warm affection for the lovely woman who stood
humbly before her. Such charm and grace and
breeding — a princess, no less! — and such a sad
story.

"Dear Mother, may I have permission to meditate
in the Quiet Room alone for an hour?"

It wasn't quite proper, of course, and not encour-
aged. Some of the more impressionable girls would
go seeking after mystic experiences and visions —
likely as not opening their silly minds to Magos
influences. That dangerous cult had claimed quite
a few who had begun by seeking honest holiness.
But Sister Halina was a mature woman and could
surely be trusted.

"Of course, my child," the Abbess agreed, and
was rewarded by a loving, beautiful smile. Then
Sister Halina thanked her sweetly and was gone,
erect and graceful in her habit of coarse white linen.
Mother Sarana could not see the younger sister's
hands, modestly folded in front of her and hidden

by the flowing sleeves. Otherwise she might have wondered why they were trembling, or why her amber eyes, demurely fixed on the ground, held hidden fires.

Swiftly, Halina made her way to the Quiet Room, the one place she could be sure of no watching eyes, no careless interruptions. And, above all, no listening ears. She couldn't stop herself from sometimes answering, aloud, the mind-messages from Valthor, and that could be fatal — especially now.

Valthor! Thinking of him, she smiled savagely. Soon all the pain and shame of the past could be avenged, all her pretences forsaken. They could strike out for the future they both believed in, and this time, surely, they must win. First the Empire of Rakath — then the world — then the stars.

Reaching the Quiet Room, Halina entered and closed the door firmly behind her. Two candles burned before the emblem of the Way but, with nobody watching, she scorned to kneel or pray. Instead she stood silently for a moment, gathering her thoughts.

A pity they hadn't learned earlier just what Guyon was carrying. But the man had shielded his mind too well, and even Valthor had thought he did so because of the aras. Had Valthor as much as suspected the truth, Guyon would never have returned to the knights with his prize. Alone, the man would have been easy prey. Now the Helmet would be carefully guarded. But not, perhaps, from everyone . . .

Halina smiled again, without mirth. Then, closing her eyes, she began to hum softly, concentrating her thoughts on the signal that would bring Valthor's mind to hers. He came swiftly, appearing in her mind as handsome as ever, proudly magnificent in the gold-embroidered black of a Magos Lord. But the sword sheathed at his waist betrayed his knightly skills. A man of power in body as well as mind.

"My love . . . " Halina whispered, and opened all her mind to him, every detail she had gleaned from her brother Kolris. The young Emperor had been quite unaware of her probing, of course. So far as he knew, his mind was totally shielded. And so indeed it was — from everybody but his sister, who had steadily and carefully opened the secret channel which exists between close kin until she felt she could use it at will. A poor earnest young fool, Kolris, so full of good intentions — but hidebound still by Codes and Creed, and so unworthy to handle the Starborn knowledge. Halina felt no guilt at her betrayal of his trust.

It was a disadvantage that Kolris had not yet worn the Helmet himself. Halina could tell Valthor only what Sir Kerouan had said about its contents. But it was enough to bring Valthor's surging excitement into her thoughts, his matching visions of what they could do if they found the ship of the Starborn. She heard his voice, speaking as clearly as if he were at her side.

"We need that knowledge, beloved. Kerouan has worn the Helmet — Guyon almost certainly has. Is he also in the Hall of Knights now?"

"No," Halina whispered, allowing him to see in her mind how she had anticipated his question and hurried at once to the Healer's tent in the market place. Still stunned by what she'd gleaned from her brother's mind, she'd had a brief, wild dream of tricking Guyon into accompanying her, then holding him prisoner somewhere, somehow. But the man had already gone.

"No matter."

There was both a threat and a smile in Valthor's voice.

"I shall try to probe his mind, and Kerouan's," he decided. "But second-hand knowledge is not really enough. I must have that Helmet. And you must help me get it. I will tell you what to do."

Halina nodded. Her heart was beating too fast, the blood thundering through her veins, but her mind was clear. For her cause, for her love, she would do anything.

Anything at all.

4

ATTACK!

Fog.

An old barge was moored in the bay near a treacherous sandbar. As the fog swept in, her crew began to toll their warning bell. It echoed through the night to the sleeping people ashore, and a few stirred briefly in their dreams.

On his mattress in the Sanctuary, Guyon woke to instant alertness as someone quietly rose and moved to the window. But it was only Sir Zak, who gazed out then turned, frowning, to resume his watch. Sitting with his back to the door, Zak could hear the least sound from the stairs, yet also watch the window, and Guyon smiled approval of the young knight's tactics.

"Nasty stuff, fog," he whispered. "It means your enemies can get uncomfortably close before you see them. May I watch with you? Though I fear I have no weapons — I had to yield them to the city guard."

Sir Zak smiled.

"Sister Zulie would scold me," he whispered back. "You're meant to rest. In addition to the zid sting, she says you have been recently wounded, and it has only just healed."

Guyon's eyes widened.

"However did she know?" he asked. "I'm sure I never told her and she never examined my shoulder, only my arm where the zid stung me. Could she have probed my mind? I saw her touch the mind of that seaman, to ease his pain and fear and give him sleep."

For a moment he was tense; the Magos had such powers. But then he glanced across at the Healer and felt ashamed. Mind-link was often an attribute of good Healers, too, used innocently to help calm their patients; and no Magos ever devoted themselves to serving the poor and sick. Even before Zak could speak, he answered his own question.

"No, she wouldn't, would she? Even when Healers can mind-link, they never probe without permission. I suppose she's just trained her other senses to tell her things that our lazy eyes sometimes miss."

For a moment both men were silent, listening to the night sounds of the Sanctuary. From behind the thin wooden wall of their room, next to the dormitory where a score of homeless children slept on straw-filled bedrolls, came a symphony of snores and murmurs. Outside, the sea lapped gently at the wharf and the fog bell rang on, in a steady pattern.

"Why did you bring us the Helmet, sir? It could have meant unlimited power for you."

Zak spoke softly, the unexpected stark honesty of his question startling Guyon. He answered without thought.

"Many reasons — but mainly because I didn't want to pay the price. The guilt for bloodshed and human suffering. I knew I'd never be able to take power without a fight. I'd have had to use the Starborn knowledge to kill, destroy and subdue people. The idea didn't appeal."

He paused, then added in a barely audible whisper, "But I admit I was tempted. I shielded my mind and got back as fast as I could because I feared myself as much as I feared the Magos!"

"And now?"

"Now I feel — at peace, relieved, almost absurdly happy," Guyon admitted. "For once in my life I'm completely sure I've done the right thing. And I'd like to talk Kerouan into letting me come along on any expedition to find the ship."

"You, and almost every knight in Rakath," Zak muttered wryly, "including me."

The men grinned at each other and then lapsed into silence, unaware that both the room's other occupants were awake and had heard their conversation.

Jon lay in a curled-up ball, hugging his dreams and his excitement to himself. If only he could go on the expedition too! Of course, he was neither a knight nor a scholar, but surely he had some skills they could use? He knew the cant and the tap code of thieves and beggars, the unwritten rules of the kingdom of the streets. The tap code was a marvellous way of passing secret messages — he'd taught it to Zulie. Maybe the knights could use it too? Part of his mind kept coldly insisting that nobody would want a disabled boy tagging along, but he told that part of his mind, very firmly, to shut up. After all, night was a time for dreaming!

Zulie, however, did not dream. She felt more as if she stood on the fringes of a nightmare. An hour before, she had been sleeping, tired out by her busy day and the thrilling news that Sir Zak had shared with her. Fear and danger had only been words, then. Her thoughts were for the Starborn ship and the secrets it might hold. Especially healing secrets — maybe even a cure for lucar . . .

But then the darkness had begun to creep in, like a poisonous icy fog, chilling her mind into wakefulness. She knew what it was. When she was young and learning to control her mental powers for good, she had instinctively "seen" mind-messages as beams of coloured light. Prayer was clear and bright; love, a tender, rosy pink. Scarlet was the colour of anger, and blue was the mind-touch between Healers and their patients, or even the instinctive mind-touch parents used, all unknowing, to soothe a hurt or frightened child. And so the rainbow of thoughts developed; but at the end of the spectrum was a non-colour, impossible to describe but equally impossible to mistake.

It was pure evil.

Zulie had known the darkness of despair. She had tasted that for herself when she first discovered she had lucar, and her faith in Yeveth fled temporarily in a storm of self-pity, anger and bitterness. Even when she had come out of the darkness into the light of acceptance and trust, she had never forgotten what despair was like. Sometimes she sensed it in an unknown mind, and reached out to offer comfort. But that darkness was clean compared to what she sensed now.

Magos minds were massing for some kind of attack, and she must be ready to fight back. Breathing deeply to control her fear, she sent an arrow of prayer to the Eternal One for strength, then began to probe with her own mind into that power-beam of evil. She knew the danger she was risking, and she was frightened, for if her own mental shields weakened she herself might be swept under evil's control.

Slowly and confusingly at first, the images flowed into her mind. In house after house throughout the city she saw men and women rise like sleep-walkers to go out into the night. In some places whole families slept and only one rose — the vulnerable one, whose anger, greed, hate or envy left a channel through which the searching Magos minds could easily take command. From late-opening inns, droves of half-drunken men staggered out into the night; thieves paused in their midnight plunders; while in the prisons men beat against the walls and bars, driven to leave and obey the dark command that echoed in their heads. All were aimed, like mindless weapons, at one place . . .

Shuddering, Zulie withdrew. She had never dreamed of Magos power so concentrated and so strong! The whole cult must be working together, with their secret followers in the city acting as a focus.

"Sir Zak!" Zulie whispered, and her voice was shaking. "We must warn Sir Kerouan! The Magos have taken over the minds of ordinary people — lots of them. They're being compelled to march on the Inner Temple."

For a moment she sensed in the young knight's mind the age-old fear and doubt of mental abilities beyond his understanding. Many good and innocent people, guilty of no crime but their natural ability to mind-link, had been killed because of that fear. But Zak fought it and won.

"Sister Zulie," he reassured gently, "the Temple

is well guarded by Knights led by Sir Kerouan himself. None of them will be open to Magos influence. And there are great minds there, too. Priest Parl is away, visiting the north, but Priest Llan is there, and a prayer-guard of White Brothers and Sisters."

Zulie heard Guyon rise to his feet, and sensed sudden anger in the man.

"How wise of Valthor," he hissed, "to warp the minds of ordinary people and use them as his army! Kerouan won't want to harm them; he'll simply close the great doors of the Inner Temple and sit tight. Even the most powerful Magos can't command a large number of people for very long. But what if Valthor has allies in the Temple itself? While everyone is concerned with what's going on outside . . . "

"Impossible," Zak said firmly. "Only the most trusted people will be there tonight."

"Wasn't Valthor trusted once? And even I?"

Jon had been listening, wide-eyed and excited. Now, ignored by the others, he got to his feet and walked clumsily across to the window. For short distances he didn't need his crutches, and he could lean on the sill as he stared down at the wharf and across the bay. To his surprise he realized the fog bell had stopped tolling, though the fog rose out of the darkness as thickly as ever. Jon could see the flicker of torches coming down one of the alleys.

"Some people coming!" he warned, and both Zak and Guyon whirled around. Zak was first at the window as the shadowy figures emerged. There were four of them, each carrying two blazing torches. Zulie could not see the blank emptiness in their eyes, but she sensed the evil flowing into them. They had been commanded to kill. Though she had heard it wasn't possible to hypnotize someone into doing something totally against their nature, no doubt the Magos had seized those who already had the capacity for destruction in their hearts. Perhaps they had been soldiers, knowing what it meant to obey an order to fight and kill. Pity and anger blazed through her — how could the evil cult dare to use and abuse people like that?

"Yeveth, Lord of Light, help me to break their darkness," Zulie whispered, and then launched her mind into a battle which the others couldn't share.

They had their own battle, and it came upon them swiftly.

The first torch hurled in through the window fell near Jon. He snatched it up and threw it out while Guyon beat out the few flames which had spread. A second torch rolled harmlessly off the roof. Even before it fell Zak leapt from the window, to land easily on his feet and face the four with drawn sword.

"Go back to your homes!" he said calmly, and the sheer command in his voice broke through to some deep vestige of their minds and made them pause. Then one of them, in the uniform of a City Watchman, dropped his torch and very slowly — as if his mind and body were in conflict — reached for his sword. At the same moment, two others lurched forwards.

"What's going on?"

In the orphans' dormitory, Apprentice Cella had woken.

"Trouble!" Guyon called back. "Get the children and patients out the back way."

"But what . . . why?"

"Just do it, please. I'll explain later."

Guyon had no time, now, to argue or go into details. He glanced from Jon to Zulie, who stood like a pale statue.

"Guard her, Jon," he said simply. Then, picking up one of the boy's crutches, he darted down the rickety wooden stairs, but not out of the door. A downstairs window gave him a better chance to use the fog as cover and creep up behind the men.

Breathless, Jon watched from the window. From the dormitory behind he could hear drowsy questions as the children were woken and hustled out; but he was more concerned for Sir Zak. The Watchman was lunging now, but clumsily; had he been Zak's only adversary the young knight would have had no problems. But the other two, though they had no swords, were also attacking him with their blazing torches. Flames lanced within inches of him as he thrust and parried and dodged in a dance of fiery death.

The fourth man, Jon suddenly realized, was creeping up close to the Sanctuary. Seeking a weapon, Jon spotted a heavy chamber-pot, picked it up and carefully aimed it. It missed the man's head but hit his shoulder, and his torch dropped onto the cobbles. Yet in his pain he made no sound. None of them spoke. Only Zak gasped as a torch seared his side.

Then another figure moved out of the darkness, Jon's crutch whirling in his hands like a stave. Guyon's first blow neatly felled one torch wielder; the second followed almost immediately. That left only the one whom Jon had injured, and the swordsman. And something was happening to both of them.

Zulie freed the hurt man first. His pain left a pathway down which she could reach, and she did so

51

with power and certainty. Just for a moment she sensed the personality of the Magos who opposed her, and knew his shock at her power. Then the Magos mind fled and his victim sat groaning, clutching his broken collarbone and staring about him in total bewilderment. Zulie did not need to see him. She knew her victory; knew too that it was not hers alone. The power of Yeveth, his spirit, flowed through her as she drove her mind to attack the last dark influence.

Zak's adversary began to slow, his lunges as clumsy as those of a clockwork toy winding down. The young knight could have killed him but, despite the pain of his burned side, he felt only pity. Guyon and Zak watched the light of reality slowly dawning in the man's eyes, as he lowered his sword and stared, stricken, at Sir Zak.

"What . . . am I doing?"

"Obeying a Magos," the young Knight said grimly, "like many another in this city tonight. Don't blame yourself."

"You'd best get your burn tended," Guyon advised. "Then I think we should leave the Sanctuary. Kerouan underestimated the enemy — I doubt if he envisaged this kind of thing — and we mustn't endanger innocent lives."

"Granted," Zak agreed. "But if we go anywhere by road we may run into more people like these — the Magos' mindless army."

A faint smile touched Guyon's lips but not his eyes. They were twin points of cold steel.

"We'll go for a little sail through the friendly fog," he suggested.

Brother Almar, the surgeon, roused by Cella, came out to see what was going on. Seeing the injured and unconscious men, and the watchman who now stood with tears running down his cheeks, he raised his eyebrows but asked no questions. He simply bent to look at Zak's burn.

"No time for that," the young knight told him. "You'll be safe enough for now, but only if we leave you. We mustn't put your patients and the children at more risk."

"There's time to apply salve."

"I'll get Jon and Sister Zulie," said Guyon.

Scrambling in through the same window he'd used to get out, Guyon ran back upstairs to the little room. Jon turned to him with wide, anxious eyes. There had been no time to be really afraid before, but now he kept going cold at the thought of what might have happened. He had once seen wooden wharfside buildings become a blazing inferno in moments. Not only that — the strange, dead, other-placeness look in the eyes of those men had chilled him. Could the Magos do that to anyone? Instinctively he edged nearer to Sister Zulie, sensing her power to protect. But she too was trembling.

"We're leaving," Guyon said softly. "The others will be safe then, and we should be fairly safe too, in a small boat out on the bay, hidden by fog. I trust we can use the Sanctuary dinghy?"

He paused as Zulie nodded, then took her hand in his.

"Forgive me, Healer," he begged, "for bringing this danger to you. And thank you for what you did. I only hope it doesn't make the Magos see you as a target!"

Zulie managed a faint smile.

"Evil is also a disease," she whispered. "But Guyon, if you are taking us in a boat — could you sail us over to the Inner Temple? I just can't shake off this sense of foreboding."

"It's likely to be sealed against the mob — and we daren't walk into their hands," Guyon protested. "Nevertheless, there's a breeze coming up now, and it's blowing in that direction. We could sail towards the beach where the Temple gardens drop down to the sea. Once we get away from the shelter of the wharf, the breeze may start clearing the fog. We could take a chance."

Zulie could ask no more. Quietly she picked up her Healer's bag and descended the stairs, followed by Jon and Guyon. Passing their former attackers she sighed, sensing their guilt, their horror. There might well be suicides and madness among the Magos' victims once this night was over, and renewed terror of anyone who could mind-link, even the innocent.

As if reading her thoughts, Guyon sighed too.

"I almost wish I'd never found the Helmet!" he muttered. "How did the Magos find out about it so soon? They must have an ally in the highest circles!"

Nobody answered him, because nobody knew the answer. In grim, alert silence, they climbed into the little Sanctuary dinghy moored to the wharf. Guyon rigged it swiftly, then called to Zak to untie the painter. Like a white bird the dinghy moved off into the fog, the wind billowing her sails as she ran goose-winged into the uncanny quiet.

Drained by her mental effort, Zulie rested in the bow. She did not try to probe now; her only wish was to weave a shield around them, a barrier to illusion and command. Both Zak and Guyon knew how to shield themselves, but Jon was vulnerable.

Once again, the fog bell began to toll. Perhaps

even the ship's crew had been affected by Magos influence, but she was back on duty now.

Zak settled on a thwart, yawning and trying to ignore the pain of his side. Jon caught the yawn, and shivered slightly. It was cold out on the water. Guyon, at the tiller, also shivered but for a different reason. Like Zulie, he could not shake off a sense of foreboding, and it centred round Sir Kerouan. The knight's trust, his kindness, were strengths that could easily make him vulnerable. He might not realize just how cunning and evil the Magos could be. Brave, gentle Kerouan always looked for the best in everyone. Guyon abandoned his first idea of simply hiding in the fog and, with the wind and the bell to guide him, steered the dinghy as swiftly as he could towards the Inner Temple. The fog was patchy now.

They were close enough to hear the waves breaking on the shore ahead when a new sound burst from the night, a sound like the beating of mighty wings.

"Down and silence!" Guyon hissed, and dropped the sails before anyone else could react. Sprawled under the fallen canvas they peeped out as something flew overhead, something unbelievably large, with the wings and talons of a bird of prey but the scaly skin, forked tail and sinuous neck of a dragon-lizard. A dark-cloaked, hooded figure rode on its back. Seeing the dinghy it swept in a circle, one wing brushing the surface of the water; then its beaked head lanced out and snapped the mast like a matchstick.

Nobody made a sound. Jon felt Zulie's hand grasp his. He bit back a cry of terror, for the creature was swooping again. At a command from its rider its talons reached out and capsized the boat. Jon swam for the surface and struck sodden canvas above him. Then strong hands grabbed him and he was able to breathe again, shielded by the boat which lay on its side in the water.

Zulie, Zak and Guyon were already there and Zak made an urgent signal for silence. Above them, the monstrous creature circled once more, then swooped again with talons outstretched to rend and tear. Nobody needed instructions; Zulie heard the rush of the dragon-bird's coming and dived as swiftly as the others. As they swam as far and as fast as they could, above them strong planks were ripped apart like scraps of paper.

Desperate for air, Jon surfaced and found himself in a patch of denser fog, which gathered round him like a cloak of invisibility. Somewhere near he could hear the beating of mighty wings as the zaarl searched for its prey. Sick with fear, he trod water, looking round for the others but not daring to call out. It seemed like an eternity before Guyon came swimming silently through the mist. The man's pale face melted into a smile of relief when he saw Jon.

"Swim for shore," he whispered, pointing to a dim line of trees looming like dark shadows through the whiteness. "Think you can make it alone? I've got to help Zak and Sister Zulie."

Both froze and fell silent as the beating wings came closer, but the zaarl passed overhead. For a moment the fog thinned and Jon saw the others clinging to a plank. Some of his fear drained away with the knowledge that they were alive. Especially Sister Zulie. Then the mist closed in again.

Taking a deep breath, Jon whispered: "Yes, Guyon. I'll be all right."

"Hide under the trees where the zaarl can't reach you."

Jon nodded and, as Guyon swam back silently to the others, he too began to swim. It wasn't easy. When he was cold or frightened — as he certainly was now — his legs felt like aching jellies. And, though he could move them more freely in the water than on land, he still had to swim mainly with his strong arms. All the time he swam he had nightmare visions of the monstrous lizard-bird swooping down to kill him. But at last his feet touched the bottom and he dragged himself up the bank and deep into the sheltering trees.

The fog was clinging only to the water now. On land there was just a ground mist, no higher than a man's waist. Above it, through a clearing in the trees, Jon could see the Temple. A crowd of people were milling around it in strange aimless bewilderment — as if they'd been sleepwalking and were now starting to wake up. Obviously, the Magos' power over them was fading.

Yet the same foreboding that had gripped Zulie and Guyon earlier swept over Jon as he lay panting and shivering on the grass. Without knowing why, he felt sure Sir Kerouan was still in terrible danger. Not from the people outside, not even from the zaarl, though it perched, silent and menacing, on the Temple parapet. No, the danger came from someone inside the Temple itself. Sir Kerouan had to be warned! In the midst of his fear a new calm and determination came over Jon. Had he tried to work things out logically, he would never have dared even to move from the shelter of the trees. But he didn't stop to think.

Without his crutches, he couldn't walk far. But

that didn't stop him. Keeping low under the blanket of ground fog, he began to crawl towards the Temple. Sometimes people stumbled into him, but no one tried to harm him. One sat down heavily almost on top of Jon, blinking and shaking his head.

"I feel peculiar," the man muttered. "Where am I? What's going on?"

Jon didn't answer. He just kept crawling towards the Temple. Looking up, he saw torches in the distance — more enemies, or soldiers called to the Temple's defence? He didn't know and felt he couldn't wait to find out. The fear was gripping him tightly now, making his heart thud against his ribs. Panting, he crawled the last few yards and dragged himself erect to beat at the great bronze doors with his fists. He knew that the zaarl might hear and come swooping down, but he no longer cared. Desperately, Jon shouted his warning at the unyielding metal.

"Sir Kerouan! Beware! Someone inside means you harm!"

He was still pounding on the doors when a man grabbed him round the waist. Struggling, ready to fight for his life, Jon turned and recognized Guyon. The man's face was deathly pale.

"They'll not hear you," he said. "I'll lift you as high as I can. Try to grab the windowsill and haul yourself up."

Jon barely had time to register the small crystallite window set some ten feet above the ground before Guyon swept him upwards. Frantically he grabbed the sill and dragged the front part of his body on to it while Guyon pushed up his legs. For a moment he thought he would fall, or maybe even be killed, for a guard inside had swung round to face the window, his spear poised to throw.

"Kerouan!" Jon shrieked. "Warn Sir Kerouan! Valthor's on the parapet with a zaarl and . . . he has an enemy within!"

Guyon's voice echoed his. "A traitor inside. There has to be! Or how would Valthor know about the Helmet, why would he be here? Warn Kerouan!"

The guard must have heard them. He turned and ran, shouting, to the far end of the Temple where Sir Kerouan guarded the Helmet, surrounded by men and women in white robes. As Jon clung to the sill he saw a White Sister suddenly reach out to the Knight like a frightened child. As her arms went round Sir Kerouan, Jon thought he saw a sudden flash of light on steel, and screamed a warning. Then abruptly the woman let go, and in one swift darting movement snatched the Helmet from the altar behind Sir Kerouan. The knight didn't move and everyone else seemed to stand frozen in shock for a moment as she ran with her prize towards the stairs that led to the parapet.

"Sir Kerouan!" Jon screamed in anguish. Then Guyon was beside the window, clawing his way up the ragged stones, clinging precariously as he kicked a hole in the crystallite. Another kick and he scrambled through, dropping to the floor inside and reaching to catch Jon as the boy tumbled in after him. Neither spoke, each reading the same dread in the other's eyes. Half-carrying Jon, Guyon ran with him to where Sir Kerouan still stood erect. The other knights and guards, together with some of the men in white, were now chasing up the stairs after the fleeing woman. But Sir Kerouan remained by the altar, and his eyes held neither anger nor fear, just sorrow and deep pity.

"Sir Kerouan!" Jon gasped. "Are you all right? We tried to warn you."

The knight smiled and rested his right hand on Jon's trembling shoulder. He seemed to try to speak, but no words came. Then he crumpled and Guyon, catching him, lowered him gently to the ground.

Princess Halina had struck with a very small knife, its hilt barely visible through the folds of Kerouan's cloak. She had struck reluctantly, as a last resort when the Magos had failed to make the crowds break into the temple. Her plan had been to steal the Helmet in the confusion, not to kill for it. She had even sobbed in sick horror as she struck. But she had struck true. Sir Kerouan lived for only a few seconds after he fell, just long enough to whisper two words:

"Your quest . . . "

He smiled again, and seemed to be looking beyond them to something unbelievably beautiful. His eyes lit up and he tried to reach out in greeting to an unseen friend. Then, with a soft sigh of deep content, the Knight Champion of Rakath closed his eyes and was gone.

Howling in his grief, Jon clung to the dead man. He became dimly aware of a young priest standing beside them, and heard the man's words as from a distance.

"My friends, I grieve with you. But for Sir Kerouan there is only joy. He is with the Lord he loved. Trust Yeveth in your pain and he will bring good even out of this dark evil . . . "

Guyon rose to his feet.

"Sir Kerouan befriended me when I was disgraced and condemned," he said softly, tears streaming down his face. "He taught me what Yeveth is truly like. Priest, be my witness now that I give myself to Yeveth, to do with as he likes. May he destroy the evil in me and give me strength to defeat Valthor!"

"Yeveth!"

Choking on his sobs, Jon staggered to his feet. A wooden carving of a blunted sword — the symbol of Yeveth — rested on the altar. He spat at it, screaming all the foulest curses he'd learned as a child in the slums. What use was any god who permitted the murder of the best and bravest man who ever lived? What use was it being good when evil triumphed?

Guyon tried to reach out to him, but Jon jerked away, then hit the man across the face as hard as he could.

"Curse you!" he screamed. "Curse you for bringing back the Helmet! I wish the zid had stung you to death!"

As if echoing his curses, the zaarl screamed from the parapet. For a moment its dark shadow swept by one of the great windows, and there were now two people on its back. Valthor, mind-master, sent a thought of such savage triumph that everyone who had even the slightest ability to mind-link flinched from the pain of it. Jon felt it too, but answered with a surge of blazing hate.

For the moment, he was forgotten. Guards rushed to the doors, flinging them open to hurl spears uselessly after the soaring zaarl. Scuttling painfully after them, Jon saw a troop of soldiers, led by the Emperor himself, firing arrows upwards. But they might as well have tried to shoot the wind. The zaarl flew on unscathed, Valthor on its back laughing as he waved the Helmet at his helpless enemies, while Halina sat behind him.

But to Jon even this scarcely mattered. Half-mad with grief he fled into the darkness, staggering and crawling, seeking a lair to hide in, retreating to the shabbiest alley he could find this side of the harbour. Until at last, under the arches of a bridge over a canal, he collapsed and cried himself to sleep.

5

PARTINGS

"Out of the way, lad, unless you want my haas to walk over you!"

Bewildered, Jon opened his eyes to see sunlight streaming in under the bridge, and a big bargee grinning down at him. As he rolled clear of the towpath every part of his body ached and protested. For a moment he sat still, his back against the cold stone of the bridge, trying to convince himself that everything had been a bad dream. The sun was shining, the bargee whistling as he led his haas past, towing his laden craft. Maybe Sir Kerouan was still alive after all . . .

But in his heart, Jon knew that it had all really happened, and that the Knight Champion was dead. Now the blaze of his grief and fury faded to dull ashes of pain and loneliness. He longed for Zulie's comfort, but how could he ever go back to her? She might have been hurt, but he had run away without even thinking about her. Anyway, the Brown Sisters and Brothers served Yeveth, and he had cursed Yeveth. They'd surely not want him back. And he would never worship any god again, or love anyone. It hurt too much.

His anger flamed again, but now it was tempered by bewilderment and pain. Sir Kerouan hadn't cursed anyone as he died. He had smiled.

Thinking about his hero, Jon began to cry again. He sobbed for about half an hour, then pulled himself upright and, using the bridge for support, staggered into the open. He had no idea of what he was going to do, but one thing was certain. He had to have crutches. Without them, weak and stiff as he now was, he'd be as helpless as a crawling baby. Even a couple of pieces of wood that he could use as sticks would do. At the Sanctuary, one of the Brothers would gladly make him another pair but . . . no, he couldn't go back. What if Guyon was there?

He would have to go back to living by his wits in the streets, and forget his childish dreams of being a knight one day. He would try to grow strong, yes — but only so he could one day kill Valthor and his murderous Princess.

If only he didn't feel so terribly lost and lonely.

Swallowing hard, Jon forced his aching legs to lurch along the towpath. Ahead he could see some trees, which might yield wood for crutches or sticks. Then he'd have to find something to drink, for the canal mingled with the harbour waters and was salty. A drink and food. The harbourside inns would be his best bet. Drunks were often generous and he could maybe even earn a meal washing up. Somehow, even now, he didn't really want to go back to begging and stealing. Zulie's gentle, scarred face, and her warning that thieves hurt themselves most of all in the end, wouldn't leave his memory.

One of the trees had lost a branch in some recent storm, and there were also smaller branches lying on the grass. Jon found two that would serve nicely as crutches, with a fork at just the right point. One was too long, so he began to try to break a bit off, wishing he had the knife Guyon had given him. But it was back in the Sanctuary.

What would they do now that Valthor had the Helmet, he wondered. What would Valthor do if he found the Starborn ship?

The night before, only Sir Kerouan had mattered. Now Jon shivered, suddenly afraid. He'd seen what Valthor could do to people just with the power of his mind. What might he do if he had Starborn knowledge and Starborn weapons as well?

It was all Guyon's fault! If only he'd never brought back that Helmet, things could have gone on as before, peacefully and happily, and Sir Kerouan would still be alive!

Sniffing, Jon bashed at his home-made crutch with a sharp stone, trying to trim it down. He didn't hear the riders until they were quite near, but then he drew back swiftly under the sheltering fringe of a weeping willow. He didn't want any encounters with the city's Watchmen, just in case they were looking for him. Snippets of their conversation as they rode past drifted to him, and he stiffened when he heard Kerouan's name.

"Yes, they've got him lying in state in the Great Temple so anyone can pay their last respects. I plan to ride over when I'm off duty."

Then the men were gone, their voices dwindling away.

Jon got to his feet, balancing on his makeshift crutches. They weren't nearly as good as his old ones, but they'd have to do. He could move more freely now, swinging across the grass. The trees were part of a bigger park than he'd imagined, and he soon spotted a fountain. He drank thirstily from its waters and sat for a moment on its brink, wondering if it was hunger and tiredness that made his head feel funny. He seemed to hear Zulie's voice, tearfully calling him, urging him to come home. But there was nobody around except a few people hurrying across the park who didn't come close or spare him a second glance.

The Great Temple. Jon felt too miserable to bother about eating yet. Perhaps, he decided, he'd forget about the harbour inns. It would be horrible to see Kerouan lying dead and yet somehow he wanted to say one last goodbye.

"Oh, Yeveth!" he wailed. "If you are really all good and all powerful, why did you let him die?"

"Yeveth gives us the right to choose between his Way and our own way," a voice said softly. "And when we choose to go our own way we often do evil things, and good people suffer. I know. I chose my own way for a long, long time."

Jon whirled. He hadn't heard the man coming up so quietly. For a moment he thought about running away, but the man's arms reached out to hold him firmly. He couldn't find the will to fight. Crying, he stared at his captor's pale, tired face, the dark-shadowed eyes and the mark of a blow still on his cheek.

"Oh, Jon!" Guyon whispered. "Hate me all you will, but please go back to the Sanctuary! Sister Zulie is desperately worried about you."

"How did you find me?" Jon asked dully.

"Some watchmen were escorting me back from questioning in the Hall of Knights. I was praying about you, and an instinct made me look back. You must have been hidden under the trees before, but as I turned I saw you moving across the grass. I was afraid you'd see me first and run away before I could even talk to you. Jon, believe me, Sir Kerouan wouldn't want you to throw away your life because of his death."

"What do you know about Sir Kerouan?" Jon almost spat. Guyon's grey eyes filled with tears and there was a catch in his voice when he replied.

"Only that he befriended me when I was disgraced. He gave me a home between my Quests, so that I was spared prison. He introduced me to the real Yeveth, so different from the cold, proud god so many of the knights believe in. He . . . oh, Jon, if I could have given my life for his last night, I'd have done it gladly!"

Suddenly releasing Jon, Guyon sat down heavily on the grass, buried his head in his hands, and sobbed. Jon wasn't used to seeing a man — and a brave, strong man at that — cry. He could have taken his chance to run away; but instead he found himself sitting on the grass too, and crying with Guyon. Neither of them cared if anyone else saw, or what they might think. Together they wept for the man who had been their dearest friend, and when at last they stopped crying Jon felt drained of anger and strangely clean.

"I'm sorry, Guyon," he said softly. "I'm sorry I hit you and I don't really wish you'd died. Where's Sister Zulie? I want to tell her I'm sorry for running away and . . . I'll go back, if she'll have me."

"Oh, she'll have you! She loves you like a son, Jon!" Guyon promised. "She's at the Great Temple, where Kerouan's body rests. She hoped you might go there, and she said she would go to watch for you."

"But can I go in the Temple?" Jon asked in sudden fear. "I cursed Yeveth. I'm sorry about it now — but maybe the priests will throw me out!"

Guyon smiled as he stooped to retrieve Jon's makeshift crutches.

"They won't," he assured the boy. "Yeveth understands and forgives, and so will his priests. Come. I've got a borrowed haas tethered nearby and you can ride with me."

So, together, they rode towards the Great Temple. It wasn't far and, as they drew nearer, they joined crowds of people, many of them tearful, who were going the same way. When they reached the square in front of the Temple, they dismounted and joined a queue of solemn citizens, most of them wearing the dark purple ribbon of mourning. Nobody spared a second glance for the crippled boy and his weary friend. The real Guyon, drooping with tiredness, didn't look much like the fearless hero of so many ballads.

Jon had seen Sir Kerouan as his special rescuer and friend. Now he realized that all these hundreds of people had also loved and honoured the Knight Champion. They weren't here out of duty. Many were in tears — knights and sailors, priests, prostitutes, rich merchants and poor pedlars. Together they filed slowly past the bier where Sir Kerouan lay. He looked just as if he were sleeping, and dreaming of something very wonderful indeed.

"Goodbye, Sir Kerouan," Jon whispered. Then he saw Zulie, waiting near the far door. Her face was streaked with tears, but she turned her head towards him as though she didn't need sight to tell her he was there. Smiling, she held out her arms and Jon hurried to her as fast as the crowds and his crutches would allow. For a moment Zulie didn't speak; she just hugged him close. Then she smiled again.

"Come, Jon, Guyon," she said softly. "Let's go home."

6

THE QUEST

The ship came in on the evening tide. Jon, catching up on lost sleep, was woken by the shouted commands of her crew and hurried over to the Sanctuary window. He knew quite a lot about ships — merchant vessels often came to the South Wharf to unload or load their cargoes. But this handsome sailing ship, with her high prow and soaring masts, was a stranger. She was a warship, part of the imperial fleet, which normally anchored in the Roads or even passed through into the safety of the Hidden Lakes north of the capital. What was she doing here?

Hurriedly putting on clean clothes, Jon swung himself down the stairs in search of answers. Apprentice Cella, working in the herb room, wasn't much help.

"It's the flagship of the imperial fleet," he said. "They're loading supplies and animals. Something to do with the quest for the Starborn starship, I suppose."

He didn't sound very excited. Jon stared at him in amazement.

"Haven't you even asked?"

"I," Cella replied crossly, "have had to look after the littlest children all day. After last night's adventures, you can imagine what they've been like! And I'm supposed to be studying, too."

Jon sighed, half in frustration and half in sympathy, and went off in search of a better informant. He found Zulie and Guyon in the kitchen. They must have found time to rest, for they looked far less haggard.

"What's happening?" Jon pleaded. "That ship — Cella said something about a quest but, if Valthor stole the Helmet, how will they know where to go?"

Guyon smiled.

"Valthor wasn't quite quick enough," he explained. "Sir Kerouan, of course, had worn the Helmet. I too wore it when I found it — I was too curious to resist. But, most important, Sir Imar the Sea Lord was allowed to wear it before it was taken under guard to the Temple. And Sir Imar is still very much alive."

"Imar's leading the Quest?" Zulie asked sharply. "I know it is his ship they're using, but I thought Sir Lorak . . ."

She seemed troubled, and Guyon looked at her with concern.

"The Emperor can't spare Lorak," he explained. "If Valthor and his Magos get their hands on the Starborn starship and any weapons or secrets of power it may hold, we'll have a war on our hands. Lorak has to organize the Empire's defences, and move against any known Magos cults or strongholds, within or outside our borders. He's already organizing strike parties."

He paused, then added ruefully: "I begged, last night, to lead the quest. I think Sir Kerouan wanted

71

that. When he died, he said 'Your quest', and in my heart I promised him that I would find the Starborn ship for him. But too many of the knights still don't trust me. I suppose I can't blame them. Sir Imar is a Knight Defender, as well as a Sea Lord. He's Sir Kerouan's natural successor."

"Not to me, he isn't," Zulie said, and Jon had never before heard such a grim note in her voice. "He's too reckless. When I was eighteen, he persuaded my brother Navathi to join him on a mad adventure. Something went horribly wrong and my brother died. It was when they were trying to save his life that I first knew I had to be a Healer. Of course, I didn't have lucar then."

She paused, her blind eyes looking bleakly into the past.

"He's not a bad man," she murmured, "and I've forgiven him for my brother's death. But he still takes too many chances! How can they trust him with a quest as important as this?"

Guyon didn't answer for a moment. He looked faintly puzzled, as if he were about to ask a question. But then he said simply: "It was him or me. And I'm not only a condemned man, I was also once Valthor's friend. People don't forget that easily. So Imar has the quest and he sails on the evening tide in a bid to reach the Starborn starship before Valthor does."

"Where is the ship, sir? The Starborn one, I mean?"

"Jon," Zulie warned, "he's probably not allowed to tell us."

"Probably not," Guyon agreed cheerfully. "But I will. After all you've suffered because of me, you deserve to know. Now, to make a map . . . "

There was a big salt-cellar on the table and Guyon pulled it towards him.

"Here," he explained, "is the coast of Rakath. Here we are . . ." He piled salt in a little heap to represent the capital of the Empire, and scooped out a tiny harbour. "Now if you sail due west for about four to ten days, depending on the wind, you come to this coast," — another wiggly line of salt — "called, with reason, the Hostile Shore. It's edged with islands and reefs, deadly dangerous to shipping. There's only one safe port — Illarth."

Intrigued, Zulie followed the pattern of salt with her fingers, guessing that Guyon had used it so that she too could "see".

"There's a small fertile area round the town, then the Poisoned Lands. They were the scene of some Starborn conflict and are shunned by all the people in Illarth, who claim that at least one monster lives there. Mind you, I've heard that kind of rumour before! The Poisoned Lands are, I suppose, about a hundred or a hundred and fifty miles across, nobody's really sure. Then you come to the Fire Mountains."

Making a curved ridge of salt, Guyon stuck his finger into it several times to form craters.

"Volcanoes," he said. "Two are extinct, with a pass between them that's supposed to be safe. The rest are either active or dormant, according to the knowledge I've gleaned from the Helmet. At either end of the mountains are vast plains of sulphurous mud with boiling pools and geysers, which neither man nor beast can cross."

Jon stared at him wide-eyed.

"And beyond the volcanoes?"

"A peaceful, fertile, wooded but uninhabited

land, according to the Helmet. But nobody's explored beyond the Fire Mountains. And the Starborn can tell us only of the world they knew."

"But the ship's there, in the woods?"

"So easy?"

Guyon smiled and shook his head ruefully, before going in search of more salt. Returning, he sketched in a north coast to the vast land, and a promontory jutting out.

"Beyond the woods, you cross a few miles of plain and then get onto that promontory," he said. "The ship is hidden in the crater of an extinct volcano at the end of it. But the promontory was once used by the evil Starborn to mine some precious metal they needed for their ships. Nobody has been there for centuries. The place holds evil memories and worse legends. It's said that hideous monsters lurk in the mine tunnels."

He paused, then added softly; "I think Sir Imar plans to sail all the way to the promontory."

Zulie had been silent throughout his explanation. As he finished, she smiled wryly. "Thank you, Guyon," she said. "It helps to have some idea of what's involved. They told me nothing, only to be ready to sail."

"You?" Jon asked, staring at her as understanding dawned. "You don't mean that you . . . ?"

Zulie nodded. Reaching out, she found Jon's hand and covered it with her own.

"Yes, I've been asked to go on the expedition," she said. "A messenger from the Emperor approached me at the Great Temple. They really wanted Parl, the priest, who has great abilities of mind-link, and is well known to the knights. But he's many miles away. I didn't tell you before because I kept hoping he would return in time. But now it seems I will have to go"

She didn't sound at all enthusiastic, and Jon was bewildered.

"But it's wonderful! Oh, Zulie, take me too, I could help you look after your patients," he begged.

Guyon's face held greater understanding.

"They don't want Zulie for her healing skills," he explained, "but for her mental powers."

"Yes. To shield them from Magos influence. I see the need but . . . oh, Guyon, Jon, my gift is really healing, and my place among the poor!"

"The Starborn ship may hold healing secrets, good knowledge that will help everyone," Jon protested.

"True," Zulie agreed. "But I still can't help feeling uneasy about the whole quest, especially now that I know Imar is leading it. I can't help fearing that he sees it just as a good adventure he can use to earn himself the rank of Knight Champion."

Clenching her fists, she got up and walked to the window. Outside on the wharf, dockers were busily loading food and water containers into the ship's hold, while soldiers urged reluctant haas and the huge catlike battle beasts, the graans, up the gangplank. Zulie couldn't see any of this, but Jon guessed her ears were telling her as much as his eyes. Commanding everything was a tall, proud knight, striding the docks with eager impatience as he bellowed his orders. Two other knights, strangers to Jon, were also there and Jon saw one strike a docker who was moving too slowly for his liking. Not every knight was like Sir Kerouan!

"Bully!" he muttered, and Zulie shivered.

"Guyon," she said softly, "I wish you could come."

"So do I. And Imar knows it. If I so much as appear on the wharf, I'm rather obviously watched in case I try to stow away!"

There was rueful laughter — and a hint of concern — in Guyon's voice, as if he had wanted to say more. But Jon heard just one word — "stowaway" — and it wouldn't leave his head.

Three hours later, as the ship swung high on the tide, Jon joined Zulie at the wharf. She had changed her long brown habit for the practical hooded tunic and trousers which both Brothers and Sisters wore for travelling. As always, she carried her healing instruments and herbs in a soft brown bag. Wanting to help, Jon ran forward and asked if he could carry it on board for her.

"Thank you," Zulie agreed. "I'll need both hands to learn my way about the ship."

Proudly, Jon carried the bag up the gangplank, then down a little ladder which led to a lamplit corridor. Even in dock the ship rocked very slightly beneath his feet, as though she was eager to be on her way, surging across the open seas. A sailor led them, opening the door to a tiny cabin. Then he left. Jon described the room to Zulie as her hands explored its only furnishings — a bunk with a drawer beneath, a little table that folded down from the wall, a bowl and a jug for washing. Then she turned to him and hugged him gently.

"Be good," she urged. "Eat well, and do the exercises I gave you, and study hard. When I get back, I'll think about trying to straighten out your legs a little."

"Take care," Jon whispered, hugging her in

return. Then she urged him to go, for the ship would soon be sailing. And he really meant to go too, until, as he neared the ladder, he saw a faint, frightened movement in the shadows. Looking closer, he saw a pale, scared face.

"Freth!" he hissed. "What are you doing here?"

"I sneaked in with a gang of dockers," the boy hissed back. "Nobody saw me. I only came to . . . to have a look. Now I daren't go off. There's a knight watching the gangplank."

Jon sighed. "What did you steal?" he asked. Freth really was an idiot. Like his friend Bok, he acted first and thought afterwards, if he got round to thinking at all. He wanted to be a thief but guaranteed his own capture. Now he held out empty hands.

"Nothing. There were people everywhere and they looked so fierce that I thought I might be killed if anyone spotted me. Oh, Jon, how can I get off? I'm terrified the ship will sail with me and then when they find me they'll throw me overboard!"

"Shut up and let me think," Jon snapped automatically. But he wasn't really angry with Freth. The boy's presence had given him an idea.

"I'll get you off," he promised after a moment, "if you promise to run an errand for me. First, take off your clothes."

"What?"

But Jon was already stripping off his own brown orphanage 'uniform'.

"We change clothes," he explained in a whisper. "That knight saw me come on with Sister Zulie, but he didn't look closely. If he sees a boy going off, dressed in my clothes, he'll think it's me. Only you'll have to walk like me too, of course. Can you?"

Freth tried. It wasn't brilliant acting, but it would

do. The knight would have too much on his mind to bother about children.

"Now. Your errand," Jon said sternly. "Once the ship has sailed, wait an hour and then tell Brother Almar I've sailed with her, to keep an eye on Sister Zulie. Repeat it!"

Freth did, and got it right. Jon only hoped he would not forget, and that he wouldn't decide he couldn't be bothered to play messenger once he got safely ashore. He watched from the shadow of the companion-way until Freth had walked un-challenged off the ship, then darted back into the corridor. Now he had to find a place to stow away. But that wasn't hard for one who'd spent much of his life dodging trouble. Little beggars who some-times tried their hand at stealing, just to eat, had to learn how to vanish swiftly. The ship was unfa-miliar territory but Jon instinctively headed out of the well-lit corridor, down another ladder and into the crew's quarters. The crew were all busy, pre-paring the ship to sail, and he crept unseen into a storeroom beyond the galley. It was stocked high with provisions, and most of the barrels, boxes and sacks were far too heavy for Jon to shift. But no mat-ter. There was also a cupboard into which things were probably supposed to be packed later, when everyone was less busy, but now it was empty. Half excited, half frightened, and grinning in tri-umph, Jon crept inside. He hoped he wouldn't be seasick, but it was too late to worry about that. He had barely closed the door and settled down when he felt the ship move beneath him . . .

Guyon watched the ship sail, waving his fare-well from the wharf. Then he went back into the

Sanctuary and straight through the back door. At a steady run, he took the narrow lane which led to the Inner Harbour. Here the smaller boats were moored in a man-made lake: nobles' yachts, and fishing boats.

The *Fair Wind* was supposed to be a fishing boat, and her faded paint gave her a work-worn look. But she was slender, built for speed, and carried more sail than any fishing boat.

Guyon smiled as he leapt aboard. He had used this little craft before on one of his quests, and he used her now by permission of the Emperor himself. There was no reason to believe that anything bad would happen to Sir Imar but, if it did, the only other man who knew the Helmet's secrets wouldn't be far behind. How he wished he could have told Zulie and Jon! But he had been sworn to secrecy.

The three crewmen had worked for Guyon before and liked him well. They grinned as he slipped below, emerging minutes later in the scruffy garb of a fisherman. This disguise, with other things he had requested, had been stowed ready for him in the little ship's cluttered cabin, and the seamen had amused themselves by trying to guess just where they were heading. Not that it really mattered. Their job was to follow orders.

Nobody took much notice as the small fishing boat set sail. It certainly didn't occur to anyone watching from the shore that she was taking exactly the same course as the proud imperial warship.

7

SHIPWRECK!

It was the fifth day at sea.

Jon was woken violently as the ship rolled, hurling him out of his borrowed bunk. The first day of the voyage, he had changed his hiding place twice: first to the beast hold, then to this cabin. It actually belonged to a man called Beastmaster Eliath, but Eliath had responsibility for the animals and preferred to stay with them, even sleeping on their straw. On the few occasions when he returned to his cabin, his heavy footsteps in the corridor gave Jon plenty of time to hide.

He hid now, wriggling under the bunk as feet pounded by the cabin. There seemed to be some kind of panic on, with lots of shouting. From the hold below he could hear angry roars from the graans and the shrieks of frightened haas. The ship was tossing like a leaf in a hurricane.

What was happening? Through the porthole, Jon could see a mass of swirling green water which fell away as the ship rolled, to reveal a raging sea.

Then he froze, clinging to the supports of the bunk as footsteps came very close to the cabin and stopped. The seamen were just outside the door, and they were shouting. Or rather, one was shouting while the other tried to calm him down. Jon couldn't help listening.

"I tell you, his Lordship'll get us all drowned, and for what? To save a few days' sailing?"

"You heard the knights. Every moment could be vital."

"Yes, I heard."

The seaman's voice was harsh with fear and anger.

"But how will it help if they all drown, eh? The storms have come early. We'll do well enough to stay afloat without trying to cut between the Ten Stern Men."

"Sir Imar has a reputation for taking risks — and succeeding," the other argued. But to Jon he sounded as if he was trying to convince himself as well as his friend.

"Who needs to fear the Magos when we've got a reckless fool of a Sea Lord willing to do their job for them?"

"That kind of talk is close to mutiny!"

There was a firm warning in the quieter man's voice and the other seaman wisely fell silent. Then both moved away and Jon emerged trembling from under the bunk. You couldn't live near the docks without hearing seamen's tales, and he'd heard of the Ten Stern Men, a scattering of windswept islands several miles off the Hostile Shore. Usually ships steered clear of them, because between the islands were rocks and freak currents and sometimes, if the wind and tide were right, even terrible whirlpools.

Jon had been going to help himself to some breakfast. He didn't really think it stealing to take food thrown away in disgust by seasick guards and knights. His stomach didn't seem to mind the heaving seas. But now he wasn't hungry, just very frightened for Sister Zulie as well as himself. How must it feel to her, being thrown all over her cabin when she couldn't even see? And if they were shipwrecked . . .

On impulse, he crept into the corridor and staggered to her cabin. As he went in she was sitting on her bunk, her blind eyes closed, gripping it to stop herself falling off yet looking quiet and calm. Hearing the door open, she opened her eyes and half turned, smiling.

"Come in," she said gently, and Jon stood still. He didn't know quite what to say. Perhaps she'd be furious to find him on board.

After a moment he blurted out: "It's me, Sister Zulie. I know I shouldn't be here, but I want to help you. We're in danger!"

"Jon!"

Pure shock crossed her face. A Magos might have known he was aboard by probing for mind-signals, but Zulie never did that; she believed it was wrong to invade anyone's privacy. And no mind-message had come from anyone in the capital to tell her that the boy had stowed away. Perhaps nobody thought him important enough to bother about. For a moment she sat perfectly still, her sightless eyes staring in his direction. He hurriedly blurted out how he'd come to stow away, and why, and what he'd heard the sailor saying about the islands. At this, Zulie's expression changed.

"I know, Jon," she said softly. "I tried to persuade Sir Imar and the other knights not to take such a risk, but I failed."

"Can't you make them change their minds? I mean, by . . . "

"By using my mental powers to override their wills? No, Jon. It's wrong. Yeveth himself allows all of us free will. So even when we feel sure it's for someone's good, we have no right to override their will. If I did that it would be the first step to abusing my power, to becoming like a Magos."

Zulie spoke softly still, but seriously. Jon thought he understood. A knight, he knew, couldn't do anything dishonourable even if it would help him win a fight which he was otherwise likely to lose. Perhaps Zulie felt like that about her mind-linking.

"I'm sorry," he said. "But, Sister Zulie, hadn't we better do something? Like go up on deck? They've got a boat there, I saw it. If we get wrecked . . . "

"We could be swept off the deck by a wave," Zulie reminded him. "Or get in the way of the crew — who might be surprised to see an extra passenger."

Jon gulped. He hadn't thought of either possibility. But on the other hand . . .

"We could be trapped down here if she hit a rock!" he protested. That would be worse than being swept overboard — drowning like a rat caught in a suddenly-flooding sewer.

"The knights would have come for me, to protect me, if there was any immediate danger," Zulie argued. Jon wasn't so sure. Maybe some of the knights, not being seamen, wouldn't know there was any real danger until it was too late. He didn't want to panic, even though he was very frightened — especially when, as the water fell back from Zulie's porthole, he saw a great grey cliff only a few hundred yards away.

"We're actually going between the islands now!" he breathed. "And we're really close to one!"

Zulie forced a smile.

"Let's just pray, then," she said softly. "Pray that Yeveth will get us through safely."

Jon remembered what the seaman had said, and shivered. What if Yeveth hadn't meant them to go through in the first place? But he didn't say that. He didn't pray either. There wasn't time before the ship struck.

There was a terrible, grinding shudder, as if something had caught her in huge jaws. Zulie and Jon were both hurled across the cabin, thumping into the far wall. Above the howling wind and the death-groan of the stricken ship, Jon heard screams and shouted orders and the screeching of terrified animals. Jon had fallen against the bag that held Zulie's healing herbs, and instinctively he grabbed it and tied it round his waist. Then, just as Jon was picking himself up, a knight with blood on his arm and forehead staggered into the cabin and swept Zulie into his arms. Water was beginning to swirl down the companion-way as he pushed first Zulie up it, then Jon, and began to scramble up himself.

The ship was badly holed, but she tore herself free from the rock that had pinioned her and plunged on, like a dying whale, to the mass of grey stone. As Jon staggered onto the deck he saw men and beasts leaping into the water, swimming with the angry surf to a flat ridge of rock at the base of the cliff. Then a panic-stricken graan rushed by him, knocking him overboard as it leapt. Surfacing next to the beast, Jon grabbed hold of its fur and let himself be towed powerfully ashore. As the graan clawed its way onto the ridge, a seaman reached down to haul him up. Shivering with fear and cold, Jon looked round for Zulie and at first couldn't see her. He called her name desperately. Anguish was already starting to tie his stomach in knots when he heard her voice.

"Jon! Here! I need your help!"

She was further down the ledge, bending over a still figure, placing her lips to his. Unable to walk on the slippery, weed-covered rock, Jon crawled to her.

"Watch him, Jon. Is his chest rising as I blow air into his lungs?"

Zulie bent again and Jon saw the man's broad chest rise slightly. He was a horrible, pallid colour.

"Yes," he said, "it's rising."

"Are his lips blue?"

"No. Sort of pinkish."

"Good."

Jon stared at Zulie, then said in a whisper: "But I think he's dead."

"He's not breathing. It's not the same. Watch. If I get tired you may have to do what I'm doing."

Jon watched. Zulie had placed the palm of her left hand on the man's forehead, tilting his head back while her finger and thumb closed his nose. She blew into his mouth.

"Tell me if his chest stops rising and falling. I need to be sure the air's going in."

Jon nodded, but didn't say anything. He was suddenly aware of a tall, handsome, muscular man towering above him, water dripping from his fine garments. The man was heavily armed and, for no particular reason, Jon felt afraid of him.

"Sister Zulie," the man barked, and there was an icy challenge in his voice, "why didn't you shield me? The Magos entered my mind and made me steer a dangerous course."

Zulie didn't pause, or even look up. Desperate to save the seaman's life, she just answered impatiently: "Nonsense, Imar! There was no Magos influence. You just took one chance too many."

The man turned on his heel but not before Jon saw the look — half fear, half fury — in his eyes. Suddenly the seaman Zulie was tending moaned, gasped in air, and rolled over to retch seawater, plus his breakfast, onto the rock. Jon stared at him in wonder. Once he'd have thought it magic, breathing life into dead people. Now he knew it for healing skill. But even so . . .

Zulie smiled.

"He'll be all right now, if someone just keeps an eye on him."

Able to glance round him again, Jon realized that many people had left the ledge. The beasts had found a way up, where the cliff had partly crumbled, leaving a climbable slope. The tall, angry knight was gone; Jon could hear him shouting orders. The ship was gone, too — only sodden canvas and flotsam marked the grave of the pride of the imperial fleet.

"Magos influence!" Zulie snorted. "I sensed none."

"Lady, he wants to be Champion, and so he desperately needs an excuse for his failure. I just hope he doesn't go talking about Magos, especially if we get to Illarth. The people there are given to stoning anyone who's different and they fear the Magos like the plague."

Jon almost jumped, for he recognized the voice of the mutinous seaman who had spoken outside his cabin. The man had come to help his half-drowned friend, but now he spoke softly, urgently, to Zulie.

"I heard his lordship just before the ship struck," he said, "pretending he didn't know what he was doing. All we seamen know he lied. But he might get the knights to believe a Magos commanded him. And if you swore none did, maybe word might get around that you were a Magos yourself."

"But how could he lie?" Jon protested. "He's a knight!" He still measured all knights by Kerouan, plus his own dreams of matchless courage and unspotted honour.

"Valthor, too, was a knight," Zulie murmured. "They're no more immune to selfishness, pride, ambition or fear than the rest of us."

"I'm no friend of our noble leader," the man growled. "Nor are many of my mates. And not one of us would see a Healer harmed, so while we're around you'll be safe enough. But take care, Lady."

"I will," Zulie promised. Then the seaman lifted his still weak but now conscious friend and, helped by some soldiers, they staggered to the top of the bleak and barren island.

"Help will soon come — at a price," the seaman said. "Salvage and rescue is a big industry for Illarthan fishermen and a bunch of them have been watching us like hopeful vultures ever since we steered towards the Islands. They also have watchers along the coast who light beacons to warn the fishing boats when to lift their nets and head for a more promising human catch."

He was right. Just before dusk the fishing boats from Illarth came to their rescue; and one day later, smelling distinctly of fish, they arrived in the port itself. Imar had said nothing more about Magos influence; indeed, he hadn't spoken another word to Zulie. He was only concerned with finding another ship or ships to continue the Quest while also keeping secret what they were searching for. Perhaps, with his adventure only a day or two delayed, he'd decided he didn't need excuses. But Jon still didn't like the way two of the knights looked at Zulie. They were older men with stern, cold, judgemental faces and the bands of high rank around their foreheads. He felt relieved when he and Zulie were off the fishing boat and away from their accusing gaze.

The knights, soldiers and seamen had all been offered accommodation in the port's fortress; but Jon felt a sudden thrill of fear when he saw the place. It looked too much like a prison. Some of the seamen, equally unhappy, had already slipped away to find local inns. "Please, Zulie," Jon begged, "let's go somewhere else. I don't like the look of this place. And I don't want to be anywhere near those two knights. They keep looking at us as if we were something nasty that crawled out from under a stone."

He looked around for the friendly seaman, but the man, who had been ordered onto a different fishing boat, was nowhere in sight.

"Please, let's go," Jon begged again. This time Zulie nodded. With Jon leading, they slipped into the maze of streets behind the harbour. Jon had expected to stay in the port's Sanctuary; instead, Zulie asked him to lead her to an inn. There she paid for their lodging, but she seemed ill at ease and Jon too was unhappy. He had grown used to Zulie's disfigurement — as a crippled beggar boy he had seen far worse. But here people were plainly unaccustomed to the ravages of lucar; they stared at Zulie as if she were a monster, or quickly glanced away.

"I don't like this place," he whispered. "What are we going to do?"

"I don't like it either," she whispered back. (It seemed right to whisper, even in their room with the door closed.) "I sense hostile thoughts, and fear. Until Illarth became part of the Empire they used to drive disfigured or diseased people into the Poisoned Lands to die. They did the same with anyone mad or handicapped. They thought these things were punishments of their harsh god, Ballat. The law may have changed now, but hearts take longer."

Jon shuddered, painfully aware of his twisted legs. He suddenly realized that he had seen no beggars in the streets, or anyone who looked like him. Did they hide in fear behind closed doors?

"Let's get out of this town," he begged Zulie. "I'd feel safer sleeping in the open."

Zulie nodded, but there were tears in her eyes. Mindless hate was new to her.

"We'll catch a bit of sleep first, if we can," she decided, "and leave when it's really dark and late, and few people are about. We're too conspicuous."

"All right," Jon agreed. But, although he obediently closed his eyes, he knew he would never sleep. He tossed and turned restlessly, wondering why things had gone so horribly wrong. Beneath him, in the bar of the inn, he could hear harsh voices, but the language they spoke was Illarth's own and strange to him. He couldn't tell if they were discussing the weather, sport or how they were going to murder him and Zulie in their beds. It was a horrible feeling.

Horrible, too, to think that people could believe you were wicked just because you were disabled or sick. The Eternal One taught his followers to heal sick people, to care for them, and to accept them. Everyone was equal in Yeveth's eyes. The sooner they got out of Illarth the better, Jon decided; then, despite all his fears, sheer tiredness claimed him and he slept.

He didn't hear the man come in. Zulie did, but lay very still, feigning sleep. She sensed no hate, no lust, and hoped it was just someone who had blundered into the room by mistake. But then the visitor closed the door behind him.

"Sister Zulie!" he whispered. "Thank Yeveth I found you!"

"Guyon?" Zulie gasped, incredulously. But at his voice her fears had already begun to fall from her like an outworn cloak. There was something about this man that made her feel cherished and safe.

"How did you . . . ?"

"A rather special fishing boat. But explanations must wait. Who's in the other bed?"

"Jon. He stowed away."

Zulie heard the man stride swiftly across the small room, heard Jon's squawk of surprise as he was firmly shaken awake. At first Jon didn't recognize the dark-haired, unshaven, tanned stranger who was telling him urgently to get up. Then the voice, and the grey eyes, finally registered.

"Guyon!"

"Sh! I'm getting you two out of here. Jon, I've a cart underneath the window. I'll help you and Zulie drop into it. There's a mass of supplies in the back covered by oiled canvas. Hide among them. Nobody should see you. One of the seamen — one you helped, I think — is in the inn standing rounds for everybody. By now I imagine nobody is sober enough to see anything clearly!"

Jon didn't ask questions. Instead he guided Zulie to the window, holding her arm for his own support as well as her guidance. His legs felt distinctly rubbery. They felt worse when he saw the drop into the cart; but Guyon helped him lower himself over, then dropped after him, with Zulie. Nobody emerged from the laughing, talking crowd in the bar and the inn's curtains were drawn. Jon caught just a glimpse of two lean, rangy haas; then he helped Zulie snuggle down between the sacks and drew the canvas over them both. Creaking, the cart began to move off into the night. Behind, Jon thought he could hear distant angry voices. But the cart moved through quiet streets and Guyon even began to whistle softly. With no sound but his whistle and the creaking of wheels — for haas are silent walkers — they rode on until a challenge split the air.

"Halt! Who goes there?"

"Gethan the hunter, from the Far Isles."

"Ah. We had word of you. You're seeking legendary beasts in the Poisoned Lands. You must be mad. Killed any legends before?"

Guyon's laugh was casual, completely at ease.

"Mad? Perhaps I am. But sometimes a legend has truth in its heart."

"Did you kill the beast whose skin you wear?"

"I wouldn't wear it otherwise."

"Why leave Illarth when all decent men are sleeping?"

"Because indecent men aren't sleeping," Guyon retorted. "There's a mob out for blood, after some poor wretches they claim are a Magos priestess

91

and her familiar. They've already killed an imperial knight. I reckon mobs are like sekka packs — once the blood's in their nostrils, they'll tear apart anyone in their path. And me — I'm a foreigner. I'd rather sleep among wild beasts than wild men."

Jon held his breath, reached for Zulie's hand and clutched it tightly. He had never believed anything this bad could happen. Had the Illarthans attacked the Rakathan questors in the fortress? If they had stayed there . . .

"See, lad? I told you!" one of the unseen men exclaimed. "I knew there was trouble brewing. I can always smell it. Ever since they brought those fools back from the islands."

"Fools is right!" Guyon snorted. His voice had got coarser somehow and he sounded just like the hunter he was pretending to be. "A sailor told me what had happened. Seems they got themselves wrecked, and their leader tried to pretend he'd not been himself when he steered his ship on to a rock. Next thing, there's a rumour going around that this woman — a Healer, I think — is a Magos. Then someone else said a crippled boy turned up out of nowhere and so he must be her familiar, travelling with her in the form of a ship's rat or something equally stupid. Anyway, you know how rumours grow. Next thing, half of Illarth is believing the Dark Lord and all his evil ones are here. And this pair being maimed didn't help."

"Don't mock, hunter," the other guard warned. "If you knew of the evil monster that haunts the Poisoned Lands, and if you knew more about the Magos, you'd know our folk have cause to fear. But you say a knight got killed?"

"Yes. The leader, Sir Imar, who started the rumour

in the first place, tried to calm everyone down and say he never meant it, so the mob wouldn't go on a manhunt. They decided he must still be possessed and killed him. I don't reckon the Emperor of Rakath is going to be too pleased!"

"Reckon he won't, at that," the guard agreed grimly. "And I don't blame you for making yourself scarce, though by going into the Poisoned Lands you're going right out of the frying pan into the fire. Still, go in peace, hunter."

"Be protected this night, guards," Guyon responded. Then the cart moved off again. But it was a full hour — a cramped, stifled, nerve-wracking hour that felt like eternity — before Guyon called softly: "All right, friends. You can come out now. Nobody'll come this far at night. Illarthans are terrified of the Poisoned Lands — though I don't believe there's much danger. Ride with me awhile. When we near the first water-hole, we'll camp and rest."

Stiffly, Zulie and Jon scrambled over the supplies in the cart to join Guyon on the driver's bench. Zulie was trembling.

"I can't get used to mindless hate, to people wanting to destroy anyone who's different," she whispered. "Guyon, we owe you our lives."

The man smiled, but Jon, watching his eyes, saw fear, pity and grim determination there.

"I was just in the right place at the right time," Guyon explained. "Lorak felt he had to give the quest to Imar — he seemed the best man for the job, and also he holds lands very important to the Empire. But neither he nor Kolris was quite happy about Imar's reputation for taking chances, so they let me use a fast boat and crew to follow. I

93

knew the course they were taking, and we kept far enough behind to be out of sight, but then we ran into trouble — some floating debris from an earlier wreck sheared our rudder. I must admit I wondered if Yeveth had got it in for us as we limped into Illarth for repairs. But when we landed I heard about the shipwreck — the fishing boats had just gone out — and I guessed Yeveth had his reasons after all."

"But how did you know we were in danger?" Jon asked. "And what about your disguise?"

He reached out to touch Guyon's splendid fur cloak, and the man smiled.

"I'd already decided to pose as a hunter whenever I came ashore," he explained. "At sea I could pretend to be a fisherman, but that wouldn't work as a disguise when I wanted to travel inland. I dyed my hair and skin while I was on the boat, to make myself less recognizable. As for the skin — it's the fur of a maneater I had to kill, once."

He paused, and his smile died.

"I didn't dare come to you when you got off the fishing boats," he explained. "It would have been too obvious. So I decided to get transport and supplies, and then find you. Illarth is a small place. I tried the fortress first, and got there just in time to see Sir Imar trying to calm the mob. I watched him die. There was nothing I could do to help him. I fled away in search of you. Mercifully, I met a seaman who'd already been enquiring after you, and had an idea where you'd gone. News of the hunt for you hadn't reached the inn, so I gave my seaman friend enough money to buy everyone drinks and distract their attention while I got you out. May Yeveth keep him safe!"

Zulie shivered, more from shock than cold. She knew they'd had a very narrow escape. Guyon loosened his cloak and put it round her and Jon.

"What are we going to do now?" the boy asked. Guyon smiled down at him.

"Find the Starborn ship," he answered simply. "Even if we could somehow get a message back to the city, Kolris has only a rough map I drew for him. Only Sir Kerouan, Sir Imar and I had time to wear the Helmet before Valthor snatched it. And anyway — a second expedition might be too late."

He paused, staring into the distance. Then he continued: "I must find the ship — and I'm afraid you must come with me. It would be suicide to go back to Illarth."

"We want to come!" Jon said eagerly. "We'll help, Guyon! Zulie's got amazing powers, and me — I'll do anything you ask, honest!"

"But if we delay you and become a burden," Zulie insisted, "you must leave us. If Valthor gets to the Starborn ship first, and uses its secrets and weapons to gain power, thousands of people could die. He's so mad for power and revenge that he might not even stop at conquering the Empire of Rakath. He wants the world and the stars. Stopping him is more important than our lives."

Jon didn't hear her. He had been tired, terrified, sick with horror, close to despair. But now all that was forgotten and he bounced on his seat for pure excitement. He was going on the most important quest of all — and not as a stowaway any more, but as a proper partner in adventure. If they beat Valthor to the ship, he would be famous. Surely not even his twisted legs would keep him from being accepted as a trainee knight in a few years' time.

Of course, if they didn't beat Valthor . . .

But he wouldn't think about that possibility. They would beat Valthor — because they had to.

8

THE POISONED LANDS

As Guyon had predicted, they were not followed. For what remained of the night they slept peacefully, exhausted, while the haas kept watch for them. Secretly funded by Sir Lorak, Guyon had chosen the best beasts — bred and trained for ventures into the Poisoned Lands. They would cry out a warning at the least hint of any threat.

Next morning, Guyon woke first, harnessed the haas and gave them supplementary rations from his varied sacks. He wasn't entirely happy about the cart — alone, on graan-back, he could have travelled at three times its speed. But only nobles and knights rode graans, and you couldn't hire them in a place like Illarth.

If only he knew where Valthor was, and what means he was using to reach the ship! Had he returned to his Magos stronghold, or had there been a ship waiting for him somewhere just beyond the seas patrolled by imperial vessels? Guyon wondered briefly if he should ask Zulie to try to probe Valthor's mind, but dismissed the idea. It would probably be against her ethics and in any case it was just about as safe as prodding a sleeping snake with a stick. Even if it didn't manage to strike you immediately, it knew you were around. Better to creep softly by . . .

The haas fed, Guyon woke Jon and Zulie and gave them breakfast of bread and cheese from his store. Jon stared in amazement at the total emptiness of the land around him. It seemed to stretch forever, without a single house. Having spent all his life in a crowded city, he found it hard to believe so much land could exist. But it was barren, except for the cluster of green around their water-hole, and similar dark clusters in the distance.

"Do strange monsters really live here?" he asked. Guyon smiled and shrugged.

"I don't know," he admitted. "There are certainly some rumours of monsters, but I doubt them. You don't normally get any big beasts where there's nothing much for them to eat. If I really were a hunter, I think I'd be disappointed."

After eating, they boiled drinking water and filled their water bags. Guyon swam in the hole, but both Zulie and Jon felt they'd had more than enough swimming for a while. Leaving Zulie safely in the cart, Jon prowled round the edges of the water-hole, at Guyon's suggestion, in search of animal tracks. Zulie was faintly puzzled — surely their Quest was too urgent for even brief delays? But she understood when Guyon came to join her. His shields were down and she sensed the tension, the loneliness, and the fear in him.

"Guyon," she said gently, "what's troubling you? Can I help?"

The man paused for a moment before answering; then he nodded.

"Is it true," he asked, "that Yeveth can give

anyone who follows him something of his own strength? His power, to do his work?"

"I couldn't be a Healer," Zulie admitted, "if it weren't true. I rely on Yeveth to give me strength when I feel weak and totally helpless. I know he'll help us now, if we trust him."

It seemed to be the answer the man wanted, for she felt some of his tension drain away, and he sighed.

"I certainly need help," he said. "Valthor's strength frightens me. When we were young knights together, he could always defeat me. Now his mental and physical powers seem almost super-human."

Zulie smiled. How different this man was from Sir Imar! It took a truly strong man to admit his fear and weakness.

"You won't face Valthor alone," she promised. "Jon and I will do anything we can to help you, and some battles aren't won solely by human strength. Yeveth will give us all the help we need."

Shyly, she rested one hand on Guyon's arm. Emotions he hadn't allowed himself to feel for a long time began to surface, filling him with both joy and fear. He glanced from the Healer to Jon, now coming to rejoin them. They were so brave, both of them — so easy to love — so much like the wife and son he had once dreamed of having. But what right had a condemned man to think of love?

"Come," Guyon said abruptly. "We'd better move on."

The day passed uneventfully, without threat of men or monsters. The only evidence of wildlife was a hawk circling lazily in the sky, and a few lizard tracks in the dust. They made good time, for the haas moved with easy grace, the more so because Guyon did not drive them hard but let them graze at the few sparse bushes in their path. Despite the trackless nature of the Poisoned Lands, he seemed quite certain of his direction.

"It's odd," he admitted. "I feel as though I've travelled here before and remember every detail of the journey well. Everything I see triggers off something the Helmet placed in my mind. I suppose very little has changed here since the Starborn left. After all, for many years these lands were poisonous indeed — anyone who ventured here died of a disease no Healers could understand or cure."

"I've heard of it," Zulie said. "It was reported to be the legacy of some terrible Starborn weapons."

"They certainly had terrible weapons," Guyon said, an odd note in his voice. "This land wasn't always empty and barren. Tonight we'll camp near what was once a town, and you'll see something of the dark side of the Starborn."

They reached the place just as dusk was falling. It had been visible for a while as a dark lump with a strange shine, almost like the light reflected from the large pool beside it, which bubbled fresh and clear from an underground spring. But the mound was black, and so was the ground around it. Black and smooth as polished crystallite.

"Intense, unbelievable heat did this," Guyon murmured, awed. "It melted stones and wood and earth together. My terror is that Valthor, if he finds the Starborn ship, will also find a weapon that can destroy whole cities."

Zulie touched the smooth surface and shuddered.

"How could the same Starborn who brought us the Way and some good knowledge also bring such evil weapons?" she asked. "Were there two races, from two different stars?"

The Helmet's memories told Guyon the answer.

"No, there was just one world," he explained. "But in its last days its people were totally divided. Some followed Yeveth. Others followed a leader so evil he may not even have been wholly human. But they only followed because of the evil already in their own hearts. Not content with their own world, or fearing its doom, they reached out to pillage other worlds, like ours. The good ones followed to try to prevent or undo their evil brothers' harm."

Jon, who had been staring in wonder at the huge, polished black gem that had once been a small town, shivered and moved closer to Guyon. This wasn't just a bright adventure any more. If the ship held a weapon that could do this, and Valthor got hold of it, everyone would have to obey him. Or else.

That night Jon had a nightmare. All Rakath and all its people were melting and flowing into a lake of shining black. Finding himself melting too, he woke up shaking with horror. At first he thought the dark shadow in the distance was part of the nightmare, but then he froze. It was undoubtedly real, and he had seen it before. A zaarl! Valthor's zaarl! But the Magos lord wasn't on its back, and it seemed to be lurching brokenly through the moonlit sky.

"Guyon! Zulie!" Jon hissed. "Look!"

Guyon woke instantly. He didn't get up — that might have betrayed his presence to any watching enemy — but stared into the night sky. Zulie just listened, with ears and mind. She seemed to sense

101

strangely blurred mind-messages, not human. Pain, exhaustion, thirst, betrayal.

"Valthor's zaarl!" Guyon gasped. "And coming from the direction of the Fire Mountains! But he surely can't have flown it this far!"

"It's dying," Zulie told him, pity in her voice. As if to prove it, the giant dragon-bird faltered in its tortured, erratic flight and sank to the ground just a few hundred yards from the pool. For a few further yards it dragged itself through the dust, then collapsed.

"It's down," Guyon said. "He must have ridden it to death. And he's ahead of us."

Zulie had already made that connection, but for the moment it was of secondary importance. All her Healer's instincts cried out to help the dying intelligent creature.

"Come," she urged. "I'll try to help it. At least we can give it water."

Guyon stared at her.

"Even dying, it could tear us to shreds!" he protested. "Have you forgotten what it did to your Sanctuary boat?"

"We can't just leave it to suffer!" Zulie insisted. "I can touch its mind, tell it that we only want to help. It won't hurt us, then."

Jon tried to say something too, but Guyon got in first.

"It won't get a chance," he said grimly. Then his voice softened and he sighed, seeing the deep concern in Zulie's scarred face, even for this monstrous, evil brute.

"All right, water," he conceded. "Left at a safe distance. But in what? I never reclaimed that useful old helmet of mine. And anyway a zaarl needs something the size of a bath."

"I have a bowl in my bag," Zulie said, "one I use for crushing herbs and mixing medicines."

"We could dig a hole and pour water into it," Jon suggested. He was very much afraid of the beast, and didn't understand how Zulie could feel so sorry for anything that had helped Valthor. The memories of his nightmare, and of Sir Kerouan's death, were still too fresh in his mind. But for Zulie's sake he was willing to help.

Guyon sighed. "We're mad," he declared. "Look, I'll scrape out a shallow hole. You two bring the water to me, but don't come within twenty feet of the zaarl. It just might decide that what it really needs for recovery is a good square meal — us."

"It won't," Zulie promised. Reaching out, she felt the beast's shock, its initial wariness when their minds touched. The only human mind-touch it had known before had been mercilessly dominating. But then its anger eased as in her mind it sensed only compassion. Not even fear, though the other wingless two-legs approaching it were afraid.

Guyon came dangerously close to the beast, but zaarls were clumsy on the ground and he thought he could move swiftly enough to escape if it found the strength to attack him. Using a stone, he scooped dusty earth away to form a shallow hole. But the first bowlful of water was simply absorbed, and even he could not mistake the longing in the zaarl's eyes. It must have had no chance to drink for several days, flying over the ocean; its whole body looked parched and dry and its sides heaved breathlessly. Ridiculously, he found himself apologizing to it as he searched for stones to line the hole so that it could hold water. When Jon and Zulie returned with a second bowl, he asked Zulie to hold it while Jon helped him search for stones.

Standing quietly with the bowl in her hands, Zulie sensed the creature's need, its thirst, its bitter dying loneliness. She could see it clearly with the eyes of her mind; the lethal talons no longer a threat now that it was grounded, but the savage beaked jaws and tail still quite able to kill. Yet had she not risked death before as a Healer? And the zaarl's promise of safety, its plea for pity, were clear echoes in her mind. Barely hesitating, she moved forward.

Guyon looked up from his stone collecting just in time to see Zulie pouring water directly into the zaarl's gaping maw.

"There," she said gently. "We'll bring you all the water you want. Now let me ease your pain."

Jon lurched forward, meaning to drag the Healer to safety, but Guyon caught and held him.

"No!" he commanded. "Any sudden move could startle it. Of all the reckless, crazy . . . "

His eyes blazed, but not with anger. He was sick with fear for Zulie's sake, yet at the same time he couldn't help admiring her intensely.

"We'll have to play it her way," he admitted. "I'll get the bowl."

But, as he moved closer, the zaarl hissed a savage warning. It had seen his sword and remembered another blade, driving into its flanks in slashing punishment when it could fly no faster.

"Not you, Guyon," Zulie warned. "It sees you as a threat. Jon . . . "

Eyes huge in the pallor of his face, Jon limped forward. He had to come within striking distance of the dragon-bird to retrieve the bowl, and his heart pounded in his throat until he thought it might leap out of his body for fear. But the zaarl made no threatening sound or gesture. It was calming now, soothed by gentle hands on its terrible head as Zulie used all her skills of comfort, reaching down to its pain to heal and bring peace. Four times Jon carried the bowl to Guyon, who ran and filled it at the lake; and three times, with trembling hands, the boy tipped it down the zaarl's throat. By the fourth time, Zulie's gentle fingers had found deep gashes in the zaarl's flanks, so she used the water to bathe them. Yet she knew she could not save the beast's life.

In its mind she read its fatal story. It had been forced to fly to the Magos stronghold and from there, with barely any rest and carrying both Valthor and Princess Halina, to this place. Not even its two huge hearts could bear such a burden. It had collapsed just short of the Fire Mountains. There, because it had fulfilled its purpose and was now useless to him, Valthor had at last released his mental hold on the creature. And it, driven by an instinct greater than exhaustion, greater than its hunger for vengeance, had tried to fly back to its mating grounds, past this pool where it hoped to slake its thirst.

"Poor thing," Zulie whispered. "You poor, poor thing."

The creature sighed, and its head swivelled to stare first at Jon, then at Guyon, who had edged protectively closer. This time it did not hiss. Last of all it looked at Zulie. Then, with a quiet sigh, the zaarl closed its eyes and died.

Tears in her eyes, Zulie moved away, only to trip over a stone. Guyon picked her up and held her close. He wanted to shout at her, to shake her for putting her life at risk; but he also found himself wanting to kiss her. Fighting the whirlwind of his emotions, he said softly: "Please don't ever scare me like that again, Sister Zulie!"

Zulie relaxed, resting her head against Guyon's chest. His presence made her feel safe, warm and loved, wiping out the nightmares of the past few days. Wanting somehow to share that warmth, yet not intrude, Jon stood close by. After a moment Guyon reached out to put one arm round the boy's shoulders.

"How I wish," he said softly, "that I could take you two somewhere safe! But we must go on, and quickly. Zulie, can you ride a haas?"

The Healer smiled, remembering. She seldom spoke about her past, but she had been born into a noble family and had once been a magnificent rider of haas or graan, holding her own with the boldest men. But she simply said: "Yes."

"Then we'll take a few vital supplies and leave the cart. Jon can ride pillion with me on one haas while you ride the other. We'll travel by night. Starting now, we have a few hours until dawn and should reach the next water-hole by then. There we'll hide and rest. Did you learn from the creature where Valthor is?"

"Valthor dismissed it just this side of the Fire Mountains."

"In theory, if they are on foot and we are mounted, we should easily beat them to the ship," Guyon murmured. "But I've learned never to underestimate Valthor. He may have some other form of transport organized."

"I've sensed no mind-probes," Zulie assured him. "So far, he can't suspect our presence."

"Let's keep it that way."

With a final affectionate hug, Guyon released Jon and Zulie, bidding Jon sort out food supplies while he bridled the haas for riding. He and Zulie both had backpacks into which they crammed all the food they could carry. Then Zulie mounted her beast and Guyon swung Jon up behind him.

"Cling round my waist and grip the sides of the haas with your legs," he instructed. "They run quite smoothly, though not as well as a graan."

"It will help your legs," Zulie added, becoming a Healer again. "Riding is excellent therapy. And I've known knights with damaged spines who could barely walk, yet could ride superbly and fight from haas-back."

Jon's eyes glowed with hope and, as the haas moved smoothly from a walk into a lope and then into a flat gallop, he clung to Guyon and some-how managed to keep his balance. As he became more confident, he thrilled to the night air rushing past his face and the return — more powerfully than ever — of all his dreams. In Illarth he had felt worthless, despised, a burden to be disposed of. Their flight from the port's cruel people had wounded his soul more than he'd admitted even to himself. But now he had helped Zulie tend a zaarl, and he was riding — riding like a true knight — on a vital quest against a dangerous enemy. Surely, one day he would be a knight for real! But first they had to find the ship.

Dawn found them well hidden among the stunted but sheltering trees that fringed a sunken water-hole. At first it was strange trying to sleep in day-light, and Jon found himself drifting in and out of dreams. But they were all tired enough to sleep for much of the day.

At dusk, they rode off again. The Fire Mountains were close now, and one of them lit up the sky with scarlet flares as it spat out blazing rocks and gouts of lava.

"Angry Old Man Mountain," Guyon explained. "Always active. The two next to it are Fire Lake Mountain and Sleeping Goddess. There's a pass between them and the Helmet says they're dormant, but I'm not going to chance it. Things may have changed in the centuries since the Starborn were here. I'm heading further south, to the Dark Sleepers. They're long dead. Also, if Valthor's on foot still, he and Halina won't traipse that far."

"What other form of transport could he get, in this barren place?" Zulie asked, and Guyon smiled grimly.

"None, I hope. I doubt if he's arranged to rendezvous with any of his fellow Magos here. They'd have to get through Illarth. Anyway, I reckon he came on the zaarl simply because he daren't trust any of his followers near the ship until it's safely his. Half of them are probably as ruthless and ambitious as he."

"I've heard that the Magos can magic themselves from one place to another," Jon said, wide-eyed. He had settled into the rhythm of haas-riding now and as they moved off again he realized he didn't even need to hang on to Guyon. So, now that all his energies weren't needed to keep from falling off, he had time to think and talk.

"They can't," Guyon reassured him, "though it's rumoured the Starborn could. They must have had a lot of scientific wonders that would seem pure magic to us."

He was right. Two hours later they met one.

9

JOURNEY THROUGH FIRE

They saw the lights first, coming towards them across the plain. Two lights like golden eyes, as if some vast predator were following their trail — but no eyes ever cast so wide a beam and no living creature ever moved so fast. The haas screamed a warning, but they seemed more puzzled than afraid, scenting something they had never encountered before.

"A monster!" Jon shrieked, clinging desperately to Guyon. But the Helmet memories triggered in the man's mind told him what it truly was.

"A Starborn machine," he said grimly. "Pray we can beat it to the mountains!"

Wheeling his haas, he began to gallop towards the slopes of Fire Lake Mountain, the nearest volcano. Zulie followed on her beast, all senses alert as she fought her fears. The thing which pursued them was certainly no Magos illusion, but she sensed a powerfully probing mind and shielded instantly.

"It's Valthor," she gasped.

"Very likely," Guyon grunted. "I should have suspected! With the history of this place — the Ill-arthans' fear of it now, their dread of Magos and talk of monsters, and the fact that it was once a battleground of the Starborn. No doubt they left some of their machines behind. Some time, in his years of exile, Valthor must have found one and got it to work. I should have known he wouldn't fly the zaarl to death if he had no other, superior transport waiting."

Guyon cursed himself silently for underestimating his enemy, but who could have foreseen this? And it was too late for self-reproaches. All that mattered was escaping the machine. It was approaching fast now; he could make out its dark silhouette, as big as a house, behind the glare of its lights. From the Starborn knowledge implanted firmly in his mind, he knew it travelled on a cushion of air — and that gave it some disadvantages.

"It can't handle steep or badly uneven ground," Guyon explained tensely. "If we can just make it to the slopes . . . "

"How did he know about us? I sensed no mind-probe until he was already chasing us."

Zulie's voice was controlled and calm, belying the fear in her heart. She was praying to Yeveth as she urged her haas towards the safety of the mountains, using the sound of Guyon's mount as her guide. But she was also thinking hard. The more she knew about Valthor and his machine, the better she could plan. Sister Zulie had almost vanished, and Lady Zuleika was back — daughter of a noble house, with Knights Champion in her lineage. A woman who did not yield easily to defeat.

"It has, I think, a means of scanning for body heat," Guyon replied, matching his calm to her own. "In a place with so few living creatures we must have been obvious. I imagine he didn't know what we were but decided to investigate."

His voice choked off and Jon screamed as fire blazed up beside them. Something had shot from the thundering Starborn machine to explode in savage heat. It wasn't close enough to burn them but, as the terrified haas reared, Jon lost his grip and fell heavily to the ground. Zulie, fighting for control of her own beast, heard his cries and felt the heat; then something like a vast, hot hand slapped her and her haas sideways. She fell clear, unhurt; but her mount had already scrambled to its feet in blind panic and was racing away. The earth was a choking nightmare of dust and noise, but through it all she heard Valthor's mind-message, clear, soft and infinitely menacing.

Your powers interest me, woman. I shall let you live while I study them.

Spare Jon and Guyon! she begged, mind to mind.

The boy is worthless. He crawls in the dust like a slug. The man deserves to die.

Harm them, and you learn nothing from me, Magos. I can will my own death.

The Magos leader tried to probe, to test the truth of her words, and met a barrier so strong that he was almost convinced. Zulie held her breath. Had she threatened him with harm it would have been a lie — she would never use the power of her mind to hurt any fellow-creature. Even an enemy. But to die . . . that he might believe. If only he was curious enough to want her alive, he might let the others live.

The choking cloud of dust was thinning, the machine's roar settling to a muted hum. Zulie could hear Jon coughing, bravely trying to stifle moans of fear and pain. Feeling truly blind and helpless for the first time in her life, she crawled towards him. She couldn't hear a sound from Guyon. Desperately Zulie tried to call his mind, but there was no answer. Then Jon touched her and clung to her, sobbing.

"Guyon — ran at the machine, tried to climb up it. Then there was — a flash, and he was hurled away. Zulie, we've got to help him!"

Painfully, the boy staggered to his feet, helped by Zulie. But they had barely taken three steps when a panel in the side of the towering machine slid open, and a man leapt lightly down. Clad all in black, even to the sword of black crystallite at his side, Valthor seemed to Jon like some demon fresh from the darkest hell. Especially as he was smiling.

"You seek Guyon? I think the shock proved too much for him."

Laughing softly, the Magos leader picked up something that lay in the shadows like a limp rag, threw it over his shoulders and returned to dump it unceremoniously at Zulie's feet. Guyon's face was deathly pale, his eyes closed; his clothes smelled scorched and there was a jagged burn mark on his chest.

"You're evil," Jon whispered. "You're wicked and evil and you've killed him!"

He tried to hurl himself at Valthor but the man kicked him contemptuously away, as if he were a mangy cur. It gave Zulie the seconds she needed; her hand touched the great artery in Guyon's neck, and her ear caught the faint, steady whisper of his breathing. Jon, his side throbbing from the impact of Valthor's boot, looked up in time to see her spread her cloak over Guyon's still form and rise, her arms outstretched in pleading.

"Spare the boy!" she begged. "Please! He can't harm you!"

"He will not be harmed. I will leave him here — if you co-operate. If not . . . "

"No, Zulie!" Jon screamed; but the Healer had already bowed her head submissively.

"Let me just say goodbye," she pleaded, and Valthor nodded. The blind Healer looked despairing and helpless as she staggered over to where Jon sprawled, and knelt beside him. Jon wept as she hugged him; but then, through his misery, he became aware that her fingers were tapping on his back, swiftly, urgently. Knowing Valthor couldn't see her hands through their shielding bodies, she was using the tap code he had taught her! Hope blazed in Jon as he decoded her message. "Guyon alive. Go on." But he didn't let any hope show in his face, and Valthor, supremely arrogant, didn't bother to probe Jon's mind. The Magos merely watched contemptuously for a moment, then hauled Zulie to her feet and hustled her into the monstrous machine. Soon its terrible roaring began again. Jon flattened himself in the dust, afraid it would run over him or spit more fire — but instead it rumbled off towards the south.

Jon got to his knees, spitting out mouthfuls of dust. He was trembling and aching all over and desperately longed for the safety of the Sanctuary, the city, where all his adventures could stay controllably in his mind. Reality hurt too much. Ever since this adventure began he'd spent so much time being afraid, and in danger, that he didn't think he could take any more. He wasn't a knight, a hero! He was a boy and now he cried the helpless tears of a frightened child. But even as he sobbed he crawled over to where Guyon lay, and a small voice inside him spoke gentle encouragement. He had been brave. He could go on being brave. He was stronger than he knew.

I will give you my strength.

The voice puzzled Jon. Was it part of his own thoughts, or Zulie speaking in his head, or Kerouan whispering down from eternity, somehow? Or was it even Yeveth? Could the Eternal One truly speak to him and help him?

New courage began to seep into him at the thought and, as he lifted the cloak which had shielded Guyon from the worst of the dust, he saw life creeping back into the man's pale face and knew he could go on.

The quest wasn't over yet. It might seem as if Valthor had won, but none of them would give up. And with Yeveth's help maybe he and Guyon could rescue Zulie and still beat the Magos lord to the ship.

Somehow.

"Are you quite sure he was dead?"

Valthor glanced at Halina, a hint of warning in his eyes.

"He should have been. The shock he received was enough to kill a haas, let alone a man."

"But did you check? Had his heart stopped beating? Did he breathe?"

"If he wasn't dead, he was certainly mortally hurt," Valthor snapped, "and in the Poisoned Lands, with only a weak-legged slum brat to help him. Do you think I should fear him still?"

Halina flinched. She was dressed in purple and gold, a lovely and menacing figure. But Zulie, who saw only with her mind, registered the woman differently. She knew Halina was close to collapse, her nerves stretched to breaking point — a woman torn by guilt, fear and new uncertainty.

"They say he can't be killed. That Yeveth has chosen to spare and protect him for a special purpose. I don't believe it, but he frightens me somehow."

Valthor laughed harshly.

"He has never frightened me. He is good enough at martial skills, but far from my equal. And his mental powers are those of a child. Whereas you, Healer . . . "

He turned to Zulie, intrigued to see that the woman now had her emotions fully under control. Her face was pale beneath the dust and grime, but she wasn't crying. At a time when many people would have been panic-stricken, this blind, sick woman was exploring her surroundings with sensitive fingers.

"A Starborn machine," she murmured. "How did you come by it, Magos?"

The man shrugged. It would do no harm to answer, for once he had satisfied his curiosity about her, she wouldn't live long enough to share his secrets with anyone.

"I have spent much of my time in exile seeking out Starborn artifacts to help me achieve my goal," he answered with rare honesty. "I found this many years ago. Some of my Magos have made a point of studying such things, and we discovered how to work it."

He did not bother to mention that the man who

had done so had become too dangerous, and had been killed.

"Why did you not use it against Rakath before?" Zulie asked.

"It has limitations," the man admitted. "It can travel over land or water — but only level land, not steep places where rocks abound. I found no way of getting it down the cliffs that surround this coast. Likewise it cannot handle really stormy seas. Also, we have only the little fuel we found with it."

"Why tell her our secrets?" Halina gasped, jealousy overcoming the fear in her eyes. Zulie smiled ruefully.

"Because he intends to kill me before I can tell anyone else, Princess," she answered. "I'm merely a disposable curiosity."

Valthor laughed, and there was something in the tone of his laughter that proved her guess correct. Halina fell silent again.

"Once beyond the Fire Mountains," Valthor confirmed, "I will test your mind, Healer. But now, I must concentrate."

"You plan to go between the two dead volcanoes?"

"If the valley is clear and flat enough. If not, we shall return to Fire Lake and Sleeping Goddess."

"And beyond? Surely this machine can't travel through heavily wooded country?"

"Wood burns," Valthor said simply.

Zulie, seized by a nightmarish vision of a Starborn ship hurling flame a thousand times more deadly than this machine's fires, saw the homes of Rakath destroyed, their very stones melted by unbelievable heat, while the people writhed in death. Guyon had called Valthor *ruthless*. Now she knew it was too weak a word. He was possessed by evil, evil disguised as a cause, a dream. He would stop at nothing.

So he must be stopped. Silently, within the barriers of her mind-shields she sent a prayer to Yeveth.

Guyon remembered pain; then sweet, singing darkness with a light beyond it. He seemed to have changed bodies, for the new one soared effortlessly like a moth through the darkness, drawn to that living, loving radiance. Then the voice told him to return. So in obedience he flew back, until he flew no longer but knew instead leaden, trembling limbs, and pain, and life, and opened his eyes to see Jon bending over him, tapping his cheeks and sobbing: "Guyon, Guyon, please wake up! Valthor's got Sister Zulie in his machine; we've got to save her. Wake up! Oh, Yeveth, please make him wake up!"

"I am awake," Guyon murmured experimentally, and was surprised to hear the words. He felt curiously unreal, as if he had woken not from unconsciousness, but from a close encounter with death.

"Water, please," he whispered, and Jon held a flask to his lips with trembling hands. The boy's eyes were pools of tears, haunted and desperate.

Slowly, having drunk, Guyon sat up. It hurt, but he didn't faint. His chest hurt most; it seemed to be burned.

"Where did they go?"

"To the south."

"They'll find no pass there through which they can take the machine," Guyon said, thinking it must be the Helmet's knowledge which made him so sure. "But let's hope they waste time trying. I feel — scarcely up to heroics, yet. You all right, Jon?"

"Just bruised," Jon said, and tried to smile. But then his smile fell apart and he shook with sobs.

"I'm so scared," he choked. "And I'm useless! My legs . . . "

Guyon felt his own strength and determination returning as he held the boy close.

"I've been scared all the time," he admitted. "And it's all right to be scared. We're fighting a very powerful, evil man. Maybe we're even caught up in a battle bigger than we know — between good and evil. I think we should ask Yeveth for strength and help. I'm pretty sure he saved me from death."

Jon nodded, remembering that encouraging inner voice when despair had closed around him.

"The Brown Brothers taught us praying means just talking to Yeveth," he said. "They said he'll still understand even if we can't find the right words."

"Let's do it, then."

Guyon, his arms still sheltering Jon, forgot pain and weakness as he closed his eyes. Calm flowed through him and he felt unembarrassed to speak aloud.

"Thank you, Lord Yeveth, for my life. Show us how to stop Valthor reaching the ship, and help us to rescue Zulie. Give us the strength to do it. Pour your power into us and protect us. Thank you."

"Help us and keep Sister Zulie safe," Jon added, then gasped and opened his eyes in sudden fear. Something had touched him.

One of the haas which had fled in panic was back.

Guyon smiled, and the light was dancing in his eyes again. Staggering to his feet he caught the beast's reins and scrambled onto its back. Jon followed.

"Thank you, Yeveth!" he said, then began to guide the haas towards the slopes of Sleeping Goddess Mountain. Without knowing why, he had a bad feeling about Fire Lake Mountain. And if Valthor was forced to turn back from the southern pass for any reason, he would have to travel through the valley between these two mountains. They dared not risk meeting him, so the slopes of Sleeping Goddess seemed to offer the best path.

"First," Guyon said, "we'll make as sure as we can that Valthor can't get us. Then we'll look for an opportunity to rescue Zulie. He'll not race away from us when the terrain is his enemy. I just wish I had energy and tools enough to dig a pit for that machine of his and lure him into it! Only then he'd still have Zulie as hostage. We must wait until something draws him away from her, and away from that machine!"

He did not, as yet, know what that could be. But as he rode for the slopes, the pain in his body couldn't deaden the new-born hope in his heart. Even Jon felt his fear and sense of utter uselessness fall away from him like an outworn cloak. Maybe the haas would have returned anyway — it was well trained and associated humans with food. But Jon was convinced Yeveth had sent it. And if Yeveth was looking after them, he'd have something in mind for Zulie's rescue, too.

"Curses!" Grimly, Valthor stared at the screen — the machine's eyes — as if he could will away the mud-slide blocking their path. Perhaps in the recent rains, the water sweeping down the slopes had brought earth and trees and rocks in its wake to form an impassable barrier. If only it had been on the Poisoned Lands side of the pass! Now they'd have to waste valuable time retracing their steps.

Anger in his eyes, he flung the machine round in a screaming turn, waking Halina who had been tossing and turning in restless sleep on the floor of the cabin. Since Kerouan's death she had slept little, for always, as soon as she closed her eyes, images of his lifeless face swam before her. And even when sheer exhaustion triumphed and she slept, her dreams were troubled and she woke within hours, tense and trembling, her heart pounding wildly in her chest.

"What's happening?" she cried.

"Mud-slide barring the way. We must turn back, and go between Fire Lake and Sleeping Goddess."

"But you said the volcanoes are still active!"

"Dormant. It will be safe enough."

Valthor's voice allowed for no argument, and Zulie sensed his contempt for and impatience with the Princess. Instinctively she reached out to comfort the frightened woman, but Halina jerked away.

"Don't touch me, you foul, diseased thing!" she spat. Zulie only answered, with pity and reassurance: "Don't be afraid. It's not contagious."

"I'm not afraid. I despise you!"

"She will break soon," Zulie thought, and knew she could manipulate the other woman to her own advantage. But that would be cruel, and not Yeveth's way. She had expected to hate Kerouan's murderess, but her Healer's instincts, and her beliefs, went too deep. She remembered the ritual words, part of her apprenticeship promises: "To me there shall be neither enemy nor friend, but only sick or well. And to the sick I shall offer whatever healing skills lie within my power."

Later, there had been other promises. When she'd become a Brown Sister, Zulie had sworn to live simply; to obey the senior Sisters and all Rakathan laws; to be chaste before marriage and faithful to her husband if, one day, she married with the Order's blessing. But these were easy vows compared to the Great Vow. That had demanded all her courage, for she knew that one day she might have to live by it.

Though men may beat us, stone us, torture, enslave or despise us, yet we will love, forgive and serve them. For that is the Way of Yeveth.

Now, Zulie thought painfully, the words had real meaning. She couldn't deliberately use this tormented woman as a weapon against Valthor, any more than she could use her mind to harm him. That would be sinking to his level, opening herself to evil. She would have to trust Yeveth.

Breathing deeply, Zulie knelt on the floor, and let her thoughts drift out to the Eternal One. She was still praying when Halina's voice cut into her mind. "Look! On the scanner! There's a spot of heat on the plain and one on the mountain slopes. Shouldn't we investigate?"

"Zulie," Valthor said, "you promised co-operation for the boy's life. Did you have other companions?"

"No, and nobody followed us as far as we know," Zulie answered truthfully. She opened her mind enough to let Valthor sense the truth of her words, and he nodded.

121

"On the plain, the boy — Guyon too, perhaps, if he still lives. On the volcano — probably their haas. We'll waste no time checking."

Halina was trembling, and Zulie sensed her desperation as Valthor swung his alien machine round to begin its journey between the two volcanoes. She had obviously been trying to delay this moment, dreading it.

"I saw an eruption once," she whispered. "When I was fourteen, my father took me on a royal visit to the Southern Islands. From a safe place we watched a red river of death flow down. We were told everyone had fled the area — but there were some boys, around my own age, who had ventured too close on a dare. Suddenly the flow changed direction, just enough. They ran but it consumed them. For weeks I had nightmares of standing in the path of molten rock and feeling my flesh burn away . . . "

"You are a woman now, not a child with nightmares," Valthor snapped. "We can outrun any lava, even should an eruption occur."

But then he cursed again, and cut the speed of his machine. There were large rocks on the valley floor, and he would have to weave between them.

From high above on the slopes of Sleeping Goddess mountain, Guyon and Jon saw the machine race into the pass, then slow to a pace their haas could easily match. After its first encounter with the machine the beast was skittish, but Guyon held it firmly under control. He felt so much better that he had almost convinced himself he'd just been lightly scorched and momentarily stunned. But he knew well enough that death — real and undeniable — would be his fate if he tried to rescue Zulie from that machine while Valthor was in or near

122

it. Even Halina, who was presumably also inside, might be deadly. There was nothing to do but keep pace with it and await an opportunity.

Mounted behind Guyon, Jon watched the Starborn machine closely and thought of Zulie, trapped inside. If Valthor had hurt her . . .

Around them, the night clung silently, the stillness almost uncanny. The haas had shrieked a warning when it first saw the machine, but now it was silent and Jon could feel its flanks trembling. No birds sang, no animals called into the night, no insects chirped. Yet the slopes of the mountains, unlike the Poisoned Lands, looked fertile enough to support small living creatures. "Perhaps they fled from the machine," Jon thought. If so, he didn't blame them. A big part of him still wanted to run away. But not while Sister Zulie was captive.

"They may be tracking us," Guyon whispered. "We'd best act like a riderless, nervous haas. But at the same time I want to get a little closer, so we can move in fast if an opportunity arises to rescue Zulie."

He urged the beast on, into an erratic gallop, getting ahead of the machine but lower down the slope. Then he reined it in.

"We'll stay ahead," he said, "as a beast would if it thought it was being hunted."

"Can't we tempt Valthor out somehow?" Jon suggested hopefully. "Or lure him into trouble? Perhaps if he hit a big rock it would tip his machine over and he'd be as helpless as a beetle on its back."

"Helpless? Not with that thing's weapons," Guyon said grimly; and as if both their minds had been read, something like antennae suddenly emerged from the Starborn machine, and swivelled to face a large and awkwardly placed rock in its path. They didn't see any missile launch out but as if by magic the rock, with a scoop of ground beneath it, quivered and was gone. Jon clung tighter to Guyon, and the man frowned. Had he been imagining things, or had the ground trembled slightly after the rock disintegrated?

Inside the machine, Valthor smiled in satisfaction. Halina, however, was close to losing her self-control entirely. "Why didn't you use it to carve a path through the mud-slide," she demanded, "so we could go the safe way?"

"There's no safe way through a mud-slide," the Magos told her. "Shift some and the rest comes down on top of you. And it was too big to remove entirely."

Had he truly loved Halina, Zulie wondered, or merely used her? Certainly the proud, ruthless man seemed more impatient than loving with his Princess now. Perhaps he had expected her to be a bold equal in his adventures, and her fears annoyed him. But surely she had reason to fear!

"Are you exploding the rocks?" Zulie asked. "I heard no noise."

To her surprise, Valthor answered.

"I'm blasting them apart with sound, as a singer may sometimes shatter glass with her high notes. Only we can't hear the sound this weapon makes. The Starborn certainly had some useful inventions."

"But mightn't it wake the volcanoes?"

Zulie regretted her words as soon as she spoke them, for they brought the terror in the Princess to boiling point. Next moment, Zulie was hurled roughly aside as Halina leapt at Valthor, desperately trying to stop him from firing his weapon again.

He had never expected her to defy him and the suddenness of her attack took him by surprise. For just a few seconds, before he hurled her whimpering away, he lost control of his machine. Skidding sideways, it struck a rock and tilted upwards, its sonic weapon firing uncontrolled power high into the flanks of Fire Lake Mountain.

Zulie, picking herself up as the machine righted, was thrown to the floor again as the earth shook. She heard Valthor cursing and sensed his struggle to control the Starborn machine and send it speeding down the valley out of danger. But the mountain had gone mad. Rocks from its torn side bounced down to crash onto the machine's metallic roof, and other rocks fell to bar their path. Too late Valthor tried to swerve again; but with a scream of frustrated power, the machine tipped over. Then all sound died except the groaning of the mountain and a new sound which Zulie couldn't place at first. Then the few words she could make out between Halina's terrified screams told her what had happened and her blood chilled.

The lava-filled crater of Fire Lake Mountain had cracked open, and they lay in the pathway of a river of flaming, molten rock.

"Yeveth help us!" Zulie whispered, as the ground shook again. Then she felt a rush of dust-filled, sulphurous air and knew Valthor had managed to open the doors, now high above them in the tilted machine. She heard his grunt of effort as he leapt, caught hold, and drew himself up through the gap and onto the slippery metal. For a moment he stood there, and she sensed the turmoil of his thoughts; his anger, his over-riding ambition — yet beneath its warping, evil power something of the man he had once been survived. A man trained to the ideals of knighthood, he was not yet utterly without mercy.

Lying flat on the metal, he reached down and called to his sobbing, broken Princess.

"Come, Halina! Jump, and catch my hands. I'll pull you out."

Zulie felt his mind reach out to silence the woman's terror and draw her to him. Twice she leapt, but not high enough. The third time, their hands touched and caught. With a powerful jerk, Valthor swung her up to join him.

Then Zulie felt the Magos leader's mind touch her own, and knew he would not save her. The power of her mind was a threat; he respected her too much as an adversary to let her live. But he offered her painless death, a mind-blast into unconsciousness that would last until the lava swept her to eternity.

Zulie shuddered, shrinking from the terror of being consumed agonizingly by molten lava. Yet some small inner voice bade her refuse Valthor's offer. She must trust Yeveth to the very end.

Then the Magos and his Princess were gone, and she could hear the crackle of burning vegetation as the slow but remorseless tide of flaming rock swept down.

Three times she tried to reach the door above her; three times she failed. By now the heat of the lava was sweeping ahead of it like a wall.

Trembling, sick with fear, Zulie sobbed out a prayer to Yeveth that death might be swift and not too terrible. She was still praying when she heard a voice calling her name. For a bewildered moment she wondered if Yeveth himself was calling her to his eternal kingdom beyond the gates of death. But this voice was human, desperate and familiar.

"Zulie! Immediately above you! I'm reaching down with my cloak. Grab it and I'll haul you up!"

"Guyon!"

Leaping to her feet, Zulie reached up and touched the cloak's soft folds. Gripping it tightly, she felt herself hauled upwards and dragged out onto the metal wall of the machine. It was hot now, the air barely breathable. But Guyon was there, touching her — impossibly conscious, miraculously renewed, and risking his life to save her.

"We'll have to jump and run," he commanded. "Hold my arm . . . "

Zulie had no idea how high up they were or what lay beneath, but she jumped without fear. They hit the ground clumsily, unhurt, and ran up the gentle lower slopes of Sleeping Goddess mountain, the heat of the advancing lava almost pushing them along. Once Zulie stumbled, but Guyon swept her to her feet again. From higher up she could hear Jon calling to them — but no, the call was in her mind, not her ears. Later she would remember that, but now her whole energy was given to running for her life.

Behind them, the lava swept into the valley, a wall of molten rock, swallowing up the Starborn machine. But then, like a river, it sought its natural course, turning to flow down the pass towards the lower ground of the Poisoned Lands. Guyon turned to look and all the tension drained from him in a great sigh.

"We've made it!" he whispered. "So long as Sleeping Goddess stays asleep, we're safe. Praise Yeveth!"

Glancing up the hill, he saw Jon sliding down to them. The boy was white and trembling, but his face was split by a huge beam of pure joy. Getting up to stagger the last few yards, he flung himself into Zulie's arms.

"I wanted to help rescue you but Guyon told me I had to stay put and pray like I'd never prayed before!" he panted. "When the earth shook the haas threw us and bolted and we saw the mountain open . . ."

Nightmarish visions flashed through his mind — and into hers. And as she responded with her own mental touch she sensed the boy's surprise, half fear, half wonder. Then the contact was gone, the brief proof of his latent ability to mind-link subdued by the power of his relief.

"Oh, Sister Zulie!" he whispered. "I'm so glad you're safe. We were so afraid . . ."

"We were indeed," Guyon agreed. "But we're still not out of danger. I won't even begin to relax until we're clear of these volcanoes and into the wooded land."

"I don't think Valthor and Halina saw us," Jon said, releasing himself from Zulie's hug and standing up as straight as he could. "I saw him catch our haas and they rode off."

"No riding for us, I'm afraid," Guyon replied. "We'll have to walk out. But we'll manage it. If Zulie and I come on either side of you, Jon, you can use us as crutches."

"Guyon . . ." Zulie began, but the man interrupted her before she could pour out her thanks.

"Dear Sister Zulie," he said lovingly. "Yes, I fished you out of that machine, but you were in there only because you'd submitted to Valthor to save our

128

lives. Jon told me. And I didn't save you alone. Jon's prayers gave me strength."

"We're a team!" Jon exulted. Then his face darkened.

"But I wish the mountain would swallow up Valthor and Halina. They left you to die."

"Valthor offered me unconsciousness so I would feel no pain," Zulie murmured. "He isn't wholly evil. A strange man."

"A driven man," Guyon replied. "One day, maybe, I'll tell you more about him. But now — let's get moving!"

Coming to Jon's right side, he offered his arm and the boy took it. Zulie took up her position on his left.

Guyon glanced across at Zulie and his eyes held all the love she could not see, and of which he dared not speak. Beneath them and beyond, the lava from Fire Lake Mountain provided a backcloth straight from hell. But Guyon was smiling.

"By the right," he called. "Quick, walk!"

Together, leaving the flames behind them, they began the long walk into a green and pleasant land.

10

THE RIVER OF DEATH

Jon woke to a soft, rustling sound, like waves breaking on a shingle beach. For a moment he lay bewildered, then slowly remembered where he was, and realized that the sound was wind moving through the green canopy above him. Opening his eyes, he looked around.

Above him, the trees stretched, endlessly inter-locked, in a sky of dappled green. The sun filtered palely through, but it was impossible to tell what time of day it was. He only knew that every bit of his body ached, including his hungry stomach.

A few yards away, Zulie was picking fruit from one of the trees. Jon had never seen the odd, reddish-brown fruit before, but as Zulie bit into one, his own mouth watered. It was definitely time to wake up! Painfully, he got to his feet and stumbled across to the Healer.

"Hello, Zulie," he said, as she heard his coming and half turned. "Where's Guyon? And can I have some of that fruit, please? I'm starving!"

"No wonder!" Zulie laughed. "You've slept for twenty hours. Here."

She passed three pieces of the fruit to Jon and he

bit into them eagerly. He was so hungry that anything would have tasted all right, but these were
really good — sweet and juicy. It occurred to him
that he'd been thirsty, too. As he ate them raven-
ously, Zulie told him that Guyon had gone fishing.

"Fishing?"

"Can't you hear it?" Zulie asked but, though Jon
listened, he could only hear the soft murmur of the
breeze in the leaves.

"There's a river not far from here," Zulie explained. "I heard it, and Guyon went to find it.
He said the Helmet hadn't told him about it, but
then maybe the Starborn didn't know. They probably just flew over a sea of green and had no idea
of what lay beneath the trees. Or maybe the river
rose out of some new spring on Sleeping Goddess
Mountain, or changed its path since they left."

Sleeping Goddess — had they really seen lava
pouring from the heart of one volcano, and fled from
death on the slopes of another? Had Valthor really
come in a Starborn machine spitting fire and death?
In this peaceful place it all seemed like a nightmare,
unreal. And yet with a chill of fear Jon knew it
had happened. Something else had happened too,
a second's strangeness, but he couldn't remember
what it had been. All that mattered was the sudden
realization that if he had slept so long, Valthor, who
had the haas, must be well ahead. And Guyon was
fishing?

"Valthor!" Jon gasped. "We need to press on . . . "

Zulie rested one hand on his arm.

"We need to rest, and to eat," she said. "We staggered in here yesterday half-dead with exhaustion.
Anyway, the river has changed things. We don't
think Valthor knows of it. The tracks of his haas led

131

off in a different direction."

"But how does the river help us?" Jon asked, just as Guyon walked from between the trees, six fish threaded on a stick he carried over his shoulder. Overhearing, the man grinned.

"Every self-respecting river has just one ambition," he said, "and that's to join the sea. I think this one should carry us towards the promontory where the ship is hidden a lot faster than Valthor and Halina can ride there. They'll need to hack their way, yard by yard, through the undergrowth."

"But we haven't got a boat!" Jon protested. "Are we going to make one?"

"Just a raft," Zulie explained. "There are plenty of fallen branches, and we can use creepers as ropes to bind tree trunks and branches together. Other pieces of fallen wood will serve as paddles."

"We'll make a fire and grill these fish, then start," said Guyon.

"Jon can do that," Zulie suggested, "while I look at your burn. You realize, Guyon, that if I had you safely in my Sanctuary you'd have to stay resting and recovering for at least a week?"

Passing his catch to Jon, the Castelmaran laughed and slipped off his shirt obediently for Zulie to examine him.

"And if I were anywhere else but in this place of unknown dangers," he retorted, "I'd make you and Jon stay behind out of harm's way. But as it is, I'd rather have you at my side."

Then the laughter died in his eyes and he added quietly: "Also, I may need your protection when we get near the ship. I don't know if I'll be able to hold out against temptation, then."

"Of course you will!" Jon protested. "You would

132

never do anything dishonourable!"

"Thank you, Jon," Guyon said softly. But then he sighed.

"Sometimes I think I understand Valthor almost too well," he admitted. "We see him now as evil, but nobody ever says deliberately 'I'll choose evil to gain power.' We both had bright ideals, our visions of how Rakath should shed past wrongs and move into a better future. Both of us made bad mistakes, but from originally good intentions. It's just that somewhere along the line Valthor decided the end justified any means. And once he started to use evil means, perhaps they twisted him. But, if I reach the ship first, might I not think of all the things I want for the world, which the Emperor might not put into action if I yield the ship's secrets to him and men like Lorak? Can I forget that, even if I return in triumph, I'm still condemned to death by the Way of Penitence?"

"The Emperor and Sir Lorak will surely pardon you!" Zulie protested, but Guyon sighed.

"They want to," he agreed. "But I know they can't. They could only do so by changing a law, and changing that would force them to give life and freedom to many other condemned men who have committed serious crimes. Once they realize that, well — justice and the safety of the Empire must come first. Even I accept that."

Deeply troubled, Jon looked across at the man he'd come to admire so much. Without quite knowing why, he thought of something Zulie had said when he first came to the Sanctuary. In those days, he had twice yielded to the temptation of stealing — once food, once some coins given to the Brown Brothers and left carelessly on a hall table. The first time he had pretended innocence and felt proud at getting away with it. But with the second theft he had felt a nagging guilt that eventually drove him away from the safety and comparative comfort of the Sanctuary, back to the alleys of the slums. There Zulie and Brother Almar had found him, forgiven him, and coaxed him back.

Now, remembering, Jon said softly: "Brother Almar once told me that our greatest battles are always with the evil in ourselves, and we can't just fight them on our own. That's where Yeveth comes in. But I don't know exactly what he meant. I wasn't very good at listening then."

Guyon smiled, and quoted from the prayer that each trainee spoke on becoming a knight.

"Yeveth, Eternal One, make me a bright sword in your hand; cleanse me from any stain of evil, break and remake me if I am flawed. Lord, I cannot be strong of myself but I trust in your strength . . . "

"Oh, Guyon!"

Zulie reached out to hug the man, drawn to him more deeply than she dared to admit even to her own heart.

"I trust you," she said. "In fact, I trust you even more now that you've confessed to being tempted."

Deeply moved, Guyon bowed his head.

"I'll try never to betray your trust," he murmured. Then Zulie became businesslike again, her hands sliding from his back to explore the burned flesh of his chest and to spread a layer of soothing balm on it. She felt the strong, sure beat of his heart and marvelled at his powers of recovery. His very presence filled her with thoughts she had not allowed herself to think since lucar came with its grim promises of disfigurement, handicap, and eventual death.

And for the next few minutes only Jon, busily grilling the fish, was actually thinking of their quest at all. Guyon and Zulie, in their silence, thought only of each other.

The raft was completed by dusk, but the moonlight was too feeble to filter through the forest canopy, so they ate again and slept on the riverbank. Jon, used to the city's wide estuary, wasn't much impressed by this small and eager stream, but he wanted to get started nonetheless. Next morning, he was first to wake. Rising quietly, he gathered berries from a bush near the river. Catching sight of his dim reflection in the water, he blinked and looked again. Was it just imagination? No, surely it was real. His legs were stronger and a bit straighter. Could all the walking, riding, even swimming that he'd been forced to do possibly be having some effect? Oh, if only . . .

Bending closer, he lost his footing and fell in the river, with a splash that woke Zulie and Guyon.

"One way to take a bath!" the man grinned, lowering his own body into the shallow water. Zulie followed and for a few moments they played like happy children, gathering and eating the floating berries. Then it was back to the raft and to business. Guyon had cut three pieces of wood to act as paddles: two to propel the raft, and one as a kind of steering oar. But the flow of the river, he explained, would do much of the work. They had no need to exhaust themselves.

All that day, they followed the river. Twice, Zulie called out a warning as her keen ears detected a change in its note, and they pulled over to the bank. Once it was for rocks through which the river flowed in foaming whiteness — but with just enough shallow, calmer water to allow them to drag the raft safely past. The second time they found the water tumbling over a small waterfall, and had to let the raft take its chances while they scrambled through the woods in the hope of catching it again in the quieter waters below. It came through with only one log torn away, and Guyon swam out to retrieve it. After minor repairs and a meal, they continued their journey, not resting until dusk came.

"Can't we go on through the night?" Jon pleaded, but Guyon shook his head.

"Too risky," he said. "There's no point in getting anywhere fast if you arrive dead."

"I bet Valthor will press on."

"He probably will," Guyon agreed. "He always used to drive himself beyond the limits of normal endurance. But Princess Halina, even as a White Sister, was used to city comforts. She'll slow him down and so will the undergrowth. Come a few yards away from the river and you'll see."

Obediently, Jon followed Guyon and found himself confronted by a web of green; between every tree there seemed to be bushes and plants that thrived on little light, many of them dense and bearing thorns. In addition, creepers wrapped their way from branch to branch in sturdy open-weave.

"Valthor will need to carve a path through," Guyon said, as they returned to the river. Zulie looked up, her face troubled.

"You know," she said, "I feel sorry for Princess Halina. How long will Valthor bear with her? She was close to breaking at the pass."

"I don't feel sorry for her," Jon replied grimly. "She killed Sir Kerouan. She deserves to have her head chopped off."

"Once I would have felt the same," Zulie said. "But then I touched the guilt and shame and torment in her mind. Anyway, if all of us got what we deserved, Yeveth would probably wipe most of us out. He's just — but I'm glad he often gives us mercy instead of justice."

Guyon nodded thoughtfully.

"I've known mercy," he said in a very quiet voice. "From men like Sir Kerouan, and from Yeveth himself. How can I refuse mercy to anyone else? Maybe if I could help Valthor to know Yeveth the way Sir Kerouan helped me . . . maybe he would change, too. Valthor wasn't always wicked. I certainly don't want to kill him unless I have no choice."

Jon snorted. So far as he was concerned, both Valthor and Princess Halina deserved to die — nastily, if possible. But he was too tired to argue. Yawning, he found himself a comfortable sleeping place on the riverbank.

"Goodnight," he murmured drowsily, and fell asleep so fast that he didn't even hear his friends' replies. Soon Zulie was also asleep, curled up on a bed of ferns. Only Guyon remained awake for a while longer, staring into the moon-kissed river. He was remembering many things, and his grey eyes clouded with tears. But they were healing tears of pity, not self-pity, and soon he too slipped into a deep sleep touched by gentle dreams.

The scream woke Jon just before dawn; a cry of such terror and agony that he sat bolt upright, staring round him, in dread lest Zulie had screamed. But she was on her feet, her face pale and shocked.

"You heard it?" Jon gasped, and she nodded. By now Guyon was awake too.

"Heard what?" he demanded urgently.

"That scream! Someone's hurt and terrified!"

"It wasn't the kind of scream Guyon could hear," Zulie explained, and the boy stared at her. Guyon was staring at him too, frozen in surprise; then he became alert again.

"Where?" he asked. Zulie seemed to be concentrating, allowing her mind to follow the mental cry of terror to its source.

"Downstream," she said after a moment. "Not too far — perhaps a mile — and close to the bank."

Jon leaped on the raft the moment she said "Downstream".

"Let's go!" he urged, ready to loose it from its moorings as soon as Guyon and Zulie were aboard. But the man hesitated.

"Forgive me, Zulie," he murmured, "but are you quite sure it's not a trap?"

"I'm sure. It's Princess Halina — alone, and she's been bitten by a poisonous snake. I don't know if we can reach her in time."

"Halina!"

Jon shuddered, unwilling pity fighting with his hatred and his hunger for vengeance. His hands slackened on the mooring ropes and he sat motionless as Guyon cast off. Stricken and bewildered, he stared emptily ahead, while troubled thoughts chased each other round his mind.

Why couldn't Guyon hear the scream if both he and Zulie could? It had been so loud, so full of fear and pain and despair . . .

"But in your mind," Zulie whispered. "Dear Jon, it seems you have a mind like mine, but it's only just beginning to wake up to its powers. You, too, can mind-link."

Jon couldn't take it in. The idea frightened him. In stunned obedience he took a paddle from Guyon and helped propel the raft downstream towards Halina — who had killed Sir Kerouan.

I have known mercy; how can I refuse it to anyone else . . .

But she was a Magos and a murderess!

"Try to forgive her," Zulie whispered. "Hate hurts the hater more than the hated."

From the river they could hear her now, screaming, sobbing and calling Valthor's name.

"We're coming to help you!" Zulie called, with her mind as well as her voice. Halina shrank from the mind-touch of one who had cause only to hate her, and continued to call desperately for the man she loved. But her voice was growing weaker now.

Guyon's hand tightened on the hilt of his sword. What if Valthor was close enough to come back? Could he let Zulie and Jon risk the quest as well as their lives just to try to save a dying enemy? Yet, deep down, he knew they must. Tense, he steered the raft against the shore. Jon was caught off balance and nearly fell out, but Guyon caught him.

"Help Zulie," the man commanded, "and watch out for snakes."

Then he was gone, his sword a flickering arc of light as he slashed through the undergrowth, carving his way towards the quiet sobbing which sounded very close now. Clinging to Zulie for support as she clung to him for guidance, Jon followed, his thoughts still in turmoil. It was one thing to want to stop hating — another actually to do it. But Kerouan himself hadn't hated his killer . . .

The Princess lay in a tangle of greenery, her body already yielding to the paralysis which would soon reach her lungs and her heart. Seeing Guyon come, sword in hand, she opened her eyes wide. "You!" she whispered. "Are you a ghost, come to torment me?"

The man smiled, his grey eyes very gentle. Sheathing his sword, he knelt beside the Princess, drawing her head onto his lap and holding his flask to her lips.

"No," he promised. "I survived. Now we want to help you."

Following in his wake, Jon and Zulie also knelt beside the woman. Her pain fled at Zulie's touch but the Healer shook her head sadly. There was no point in going through the motions, in trying to suck out the venom. It had already spread too far.

"I'm sorry," she said softly. "I can't save you. But . . ."

The Princess didn't seem to hear them. Her eyes looked beyond them, bleak with misery.

"I was too tired to go on," she murmured. "Valthor left me in a clearing, where there was food and water. He said I'd be safe there until he returned. But I'm not used to the forest — all the noises in the night — the eyes watching me. I tried to follow the way he'd gone but . . ."

She paused, shuddering, and Zulie soothed her wordlessly.

"It was such a little snake. I trod on it before I saw it and it struck me. I called to Valthor but he didn't answer me. I couldn't reach his mind."

Her breathing was shallow and laboured now, her eyes bright with anguish.

"Yeveth forgive me!" she whispered. "I've been

evil — all my bright dreams just evil shadows —
oh, if only . . . "

They were the saddest words Jon had ever heard,
and the last bit of his hatred melted away. He hoped
he'd never have to end his life wishing with all his
heart that he'd done things differently. He was glad
that Guyon kept holding Halina gently, stroking her
hair with his strong swordsman's hand. But most
of all Jon wished he had the power to help the
woman who lay dying. Zulie understood without
words and, taking his hand, placed it on top of her
own, on Halina's forehead.

"Think of peace," she urged, "of beauty, forgive-
ness and welcome. Ask Yeveth to help us bring her
sleep, free from pain, so that she slips gently into
death."

Jon nodded. His young life hadn't yielded many
real experiences of peace and beauty, but he could
think of the security and affection he'd found with
the Brown Brothers and Sisters. And he did forgive.
He let it all flow from him.

Halina sighed softly and closed her eyes, drifting
gently into dreams. All the lines melted from her
proud copper face and she lay innocently beautiful,
smiling faintly. Then Zulie drew Jon's hand away,
for it was all over. Healer and boy stared at each
other, and Zulie spoke first.

"Thank you, Jon," she whispered. "You helped
to bring her peace, and you helped me too. Yeveth
has given you a wonderful gift and we never even
realized!"

Jon didn't understand what had happened, but
he knew something had. It made him feel strangely
happy yet, at the same time, frightened. Not knowing what to say, he stood up silently and was

glad when Guyon also rose and gave him a job to do.

"We daren't risk a funeral pyre, not in this dense forest," the Castelmaran said. "And we've nothing to dig a grave with. But we can pile stones over her body, so the scavengers don't get it. Then we must move on."

Working swiftly, Guyon and Jon hunted out stones while Zulie formed them into a cairn. When it was done, Zulie murmured a prayer, and made the blunt-sword emblem of the Way out of two twigs.

There was no point in resting any more. Following the path Guyon had carved, they made their way back to the raft in thoughtful silence and piled aboard. In the canopy of the forest above them, daylight creatures were greeting the morning with a symphony of chittering cries and birdsong. They could pluck and eat ripe fruits from overhanging branches as they paddled, and flowers scented the air. In this place, it seemed, there were no seasons. It was beautiful, colourful, peaceful — yet it held poisonous snakes.

And they still had to face Valthor, who was deadlier by far.

11

TRICKERY

Jon paddled automatically, lost in his thoughts. He had left the city a streetwise boy, but he felt much older now. Frightened, too. Nothing was certain any more, not even his daydreams of becoming a knight. Somehow when he had tried to ease Princess Halina's pain it had felt so very right, as if that was what he was born to do.

Zulie, understanding his confusion, paused in her paddling to hug him. But she too was troubled.

"I think Valthor will know we're here, now," she murmured. "He couldn't fail to sense the help we gave to Princess Halina."

Jon in particular, with his untrained new power, would have stood out like a beacon. But she didn't say so. The boy's thoughts were troubled enough already.

"If he knows about us surviving, he may also know how we are travelling — and could ambush us," Guyon said grimly, steering the raft into the bank. He wondered what weapons the Magos lord had. Against a sword they'd be safe enough, but arrows, or spears, or throwing stars could pluck them from the exposed raft as easily as they plucked fruit from the trees. But to carve their way through the forest would be slow and dangerous, and could give Valthor the advantage again. They had to stay on the river.

"We'll stop for a while," Guyon decided, "and make some kind of cabin for the raft. Something as arrow-proof as possible. Jon, you keep watch while I go and gather branches and Zulie helps tie them together. We'll use vines as rope again."

They worked in grim silence, broken only once by Jon's soft question.

"Did we do wrong to help Princess Halina, then? If we hadn't . . . "

"No," Zulie said firmly. "We did right! If we'd ignored her need, even for the sake of the ship — that would have been wrong."

"We'd also have spent a lot of time feeling guilty and miserable, when we need to feel alert and confident," Guyon agreed, as he staggered back under the weight of an armful of logs. "Don't worry. We'll beat Valthor yet. We're more rested than he is, for a start. And he has the Helmet. That could work to our advantage."

"What do you mean?"

"Because he can wear it whenever he wants to check up on things, he's likely to trust it implicitly," Guyon explained. "He missed this river, because the Helmet didn't mention it. We found it, because I was willing to listen to Zulie when she heard it. There might be other things we discover which he misses simply because he doesn't expect to find them."

He only wished he could feel as confident as he made himself sound, for in reality he was very much afraid. The closer he came to his goal, the more ruthless Valthor was likely to become — perhaps out of sheer desperation. For if Valthor failed in this quest, he might well lose the leadership of the Magos. The proud sect didn't tolerate failures gladly. Then how could he pursue his dreams?

But if he reached the ship first . . .

Guyon shuddered as images came to him of war beyond any nightmare. No, not even war, because that implied combat between equal forces. If the ship held Starborn weapons, there could be destruction, merciless and terrible, until the whole world surrendered to Valthor's rule. As Guyon helped Zulie bind the logs together into a basic box-shaped cabin, he wished that somehow the clock could be turned back and history changed. Things would be so very different if only Sir Kerouan had lived to lead the quest.

"I'm not equal to the task, Lord," he admitted silently; and he felt reassurance, unspoken and indefinable, touch him like a caress, promising him that his own weakness didn't matter.

"Yeveth?"

He looked up, glancing round as if he half expected to find the Eternal One standing there, watching, smiling. But there were only Zulie and Jon, and the plants, trees and creatures of the forest to be seen. Yet Yeveth was there, he knew; while something dark, evil and infinitely threatening loomed and seemed to have Valthor in its grip. Without knowing why, Guyon felt sure that this was no mere race between human beings for a Starborn ship. It was a fragment of a challenge that had raged almost since the beginning of time, and across the whole created universe.

As Guyon rose to seek out the last few branches

needed for their makeshift cabin, in his heart he reached out to Yeveth.

"You know I am yours now, Lord. Do with me as you will."

Then, feeling the beginnings of a new, deep peace, he went back to complete the cabin. It was hardly a masterpiece of design, or of strength. In fact, it was a box of logs with a door, and slots that served both as windows and spaces through which the paddles could stick out. But it was protection. Guyon carefully drenched the whole thing in case Valthor chose to use fire arrows. Then they set off again, through forest which seemed to be becoming less dense. After a couple of hours, the banks began to steepen.

"If Valthor's going to ambush us," Guyon warned, "I think he'll choose to do so soon."

A quarter of an hour later, Zulie frowned.

"Can we pull into the bank, Guyon? I think the note of the river is changing."

Obediently, Guyon steered for the shore and, hiding the raft as best he could under an overhanging tree, he slipped ashore to scout downstream. Of necessity he had learned stealth and made as little noise as a wild creature. Here few bushes and creepers barred his way, and from the higher bank it was easy to climb a tree that gave a good view downstream.

Zulie was right about the river — its note was changing as it split into two. One stream flowed slightly east of north, by Guyon's calculations; the other, narrower one flowed due north, down between steep rocky banks. It was faster and looked more treacherous. Obviously the right-hand fork would be better — but for one important factor.

Valthor was waiting just a short way down its banks.

Guyon couldn't see the Magos leader, but a flock of small birds angrily scolding from the higher branches betrayed some threat. In a muddy part of the bank near the river's fork, he could clearly see the tracks of a haas. Careless of Valthor not to have noticed, but then he'd been hacking his way through undergrowth for ages and had to be tired. Perhaps tired enough to make mistakes.

As silently as he'd come, Guyon crept back to join the others and tell them what he had seen. It troubled him slightly that the Helmet's memories still gave him no guidance about the river; the only river they mentioned was not in the woodlands, but made its way across the plain. Either they hadn't thought it important enough to mention, or he had lost some of the Helmet's gift of knowledge through his period of unconsciousness.

"But even if I knew exactly where the rivers went," he said ruefully, "I don't think we have a choice. We want to avoid Valthor if we possibly can. We've no means of knowing if he carries some Starborn hand weapons taken from that machine of his."

"The left-hand fork sounds more dangerous, but I feel we should take it," Zulie agreed. "What worries me is that Valthor isn't trying his mind powers out on us — though he is shielding."

"Maybe that's a luxury he dares allow himself only when he feels he's winning," Guyon guessed.

"I bet he daren't, Zulie! He knows how strong your powers are!" Jon said loyally.

Zulie shook her head, sure that wasn't the answer, though touched by Jon's trust. She had a nasty feeling that Valthor was plotting something sinister, yet at the same time her prayers to Yeveth gave her a sense of reassurance.

"The north stream," she said softly. "Whatever dangers it holds, Yeveth is with us."

"Let's go, then."

Guyon and Zulie paddled this time, while Jon held the steering oar. He was glad to have something practical to blank out his rising fear. Through the slit in the logs he saw the fork in the river and, helped by Guyon, steered the raft resolutely left. Just for a moment he saw a black-clad figure race from cover on the bank of the right-hand fork, raise a bow and fire. Two arrows thudded harmlessly into the makeshift wooden cabin before the raft was swept on, between the shielding banks, going faster now so that paddling was unnecessary.

Left behind on the bank, the man in black began to laugh, a cruel and terrible sound. How very easily they had been fooled into rushing to their own destruction! Soon they would see what he had seen, scouting the area a few hours before. But by the time they saw their danger, it would be far too late.

12

LABYRINTH

One moment they were speeding down a rocky cleft, with thinning trees above them. Next moment the hill was there, its mouth open to swallow them up. There was no ledge, no overhanging branch to grab; and when Guyon tried to wedge his paddle against the walls of rock, it simply snapped in his hands as the force of the water bore them on. Jon didn't have time even to scream before they were swept into darkness, and the roar of water echoed from cavern walls.

"Forgive me!" Guyon whispered; then he spent no more time on shame or guilt. That could come later. Right now they were still alive and had to stay that way. Stripping off his tunic, he wound it round the broken paddle to make a torch. After several attempts with his flints he managed to light it, and kicked open the door of the cabin to survey his surroundings. Jon and Zulie followed.

They were in a vast, long cave, too regular surely to have been carved by nature alone. No light crept in — they had been swept too far from the cave's mouth — but the air was still fresh. Somewhere ahead the water thundered in a new and menacing way. Handing the makeshift torch to Jon, Guyon took his paddle and rapidly steered the raft to shore. Soon they all stood trembling on rock ledges.

For a while nobody spoke. Jon knew he would burst into tears if he tried to say a word, and Zulie, herself badly shaken, reached out to comfort him. Guyon held them both, his grey eyes tear-bright. He was the first to find words.

"I'm sorry," he said. "I'd forgotten just how cunning Valthor is. He obviously meant me to suspect his presence. He must have known what lay ahead and tricked us into going the way he wanted."

"No, Guyon," Zulie replied, and in the red glow of the torch Guyon saw that her face held neither fear nor blame, but only love.

"You mustn't blame yourself for anything!" she insisted. "I honestly believe this is the way Yeveth wanted us to come. Don't ask me why, because I don't know."

Jon found his voice at last, though it still quavered perilously on the brink of tears.

"But where are we?" he asked. "And how do we get out?"

Guyon closed his eyes, trying to concentrate on the Helmet memories. But it was Zulie who suggested, almost shyly, "Could we already be underneath the promontory where the ship is?"

Wide-eyed, Guyon stared at her.

"But the woodlands didn't extend to the coast! There was a plain between . . . "

He paused to grab the torch from Jon and drop it before the last flaming scrap of cloth could fall loose and burn the boy. Out of the darkness, Zulie's voice continued, "Remember the map you drew with salt on our table? You didn't mention any hill in the woods. But wasn't the promontory itself higher ground? Surely it must have been, if it was an old volcano."

"Of course! It rose out of the strip of plain between the forest and the coast. And with no people around for centuries the forest could have spread . . . "

Listening, Jon caught the warmth of their excitement, but couldn't quite share it. He had almost come to the end of his courage and this dead underground darkness, so different from the half-darkness of the city whose dangers he knew, terrified him. He kept sensing things moving in the black unknown. A knight, he told himself fiercely, wouldn't be scared of the dark. A knight would press on to complete his quest in triumph. But he wasn't a knight. He was a boy who no longer felt he even knew who he really was or would be — if he lived. He felt small and very much afraid.

"Please," he begged, "please, Guyon, can we have a torch again? I hate this darkness!"

He hated the whimper in his voice, but it wouldn't go away. Nor would the tears. Try as he might, all his fears suddenly overflowed like a bursting dam and he wept, his sobs echoing in the cave. When Zulie reached out to hold him close, he didn't resist.

"My dear, brave friends," Guyon murmured, jumping back onto the raft for another paddle. He had lost his cloak long before, but Zulie tore a wide strip of fabric from the hem of her robes, so soon another torch sent its comforting glow into the darkness, and found a luminous reflection further down the cave. Whatever the light had touched scuttled back into the darkness, and Guyon remembered the legends of monsters in the old Starborn mines.

"Yeveth, help me!" he prayed silently. "I led my friends into this danger — help me to get them out!"

Even as he prayed, the Helmet memories began to filter back into his mind, like a soft voice speaking from the past. They had mentioned a river crossing the plains. The evil Starborn had diverted some of the water, carving an underground canal which swept over a natural fall to provide something they called hydroelectric power. When they had freed the people enslaved here, the good Starborn had left some of that power working for whoever might one day come to seek their ship.

Clothes do not make long-lasting torches. In the last light from his, Guyon searched the wall for what his Starborn memories now urged him to find. They were almost in darkness again when his fingers touched something that was not rock. He pressed it and the cavern flooded with pale, golden light.

Breathing a deep sigh of relief, he turned to Jon and Zulie. Whatever the creatures were that lived in the old mine workings, they were used to darkness. While the light lasted, they should keep away.

"We are indeed under the promontory," he said. "This light is a legacy from the Starborn. Can you bear to go on, just till we find a way out? Not too far ahead there should be a side tunnel, leading to a cave in the cliffs. We'll demolish the raft and use the creepers binding it as a rope, in case any climbing is involved."

Jon knew the question was really for him. Could he go on? All his fears and doubts still surged inside him like a raging sea, but over it all he heard that soft reassuring voice again. *You are stronger than you know . . . I will be your strength.*

He took a deep breath.

"Yes, Guyon. I can go on. Let's find the ship!"

"Lead on, Guyon!" Zulie agreed, smiling.

First they hauled the raft onto the ledge and untied the logs, leaving them there in a pile. Guyon did not know what kind of Starborn machinery made light from falling water, but he didn't want to chance its being wrecked by logs. Then, selecting several lighter branches, he turned to Jon.

"Would sticks or crutches help you?"

"I'm faster with crutches," the boy agreed. "And I can use them as weapons."

With his sword, Guyon roughly shaped two branches, strapping on extra pieces for grips. Testing them on the ledge, Jon felt some of his old excitement returning. For himself, Guyon carved a branch to be both staff and spear, giving a far longer reach than his sword. Then it was time to move on. With Zulie gently holding his left arm for guidance, Guyon led them further into the cave.

The river was truly roaring now, and a rainbow coloured cloud of spray showed where it dropped down a pothole. Perhaps later they would discover the Starborn machinery and learn how it worked, but now Guyon was eager to get on.

It wouldn't take Valthor long to realize his mistake, he decided. The moment he spotted the sea he would realize he had been waiting to cross a plain that no longer existed, and would recognize the promontory for what it was. Then of course he had only to ride across to it, and he could travel much faster on haas-back above than they could scramble through the caves below. Fury at his mistake would probably give him wings!

Guyon shivered as ice-cold, nameless fear caught

his soul. In every side tunnel he could sense the creatures that were waiting and knew they would come surging out if the light should fail. Ahead of him, tiny droplets of rainbow light hung suspended in mid-air and when he thrust his pole forward it struck an almost invisible tracery of web. As he tore it away from the walls a fragment fell on his bare arm, burning him as if it had been dipped in acid. He said nothing; Jon hadn't seen it and he didn't want to add any more to the boy's burden of fear. Poor lad, he'd been so very brave, but he set himself too high a target of fearlessness and felt ashamed when terror came. Only a few people were truly fearless, Guyon knew, and sometimes it wasn't a good thing to be. Valthor had never admitted to fear or indeed to any other weakness.

Guyon shivered. In this strange and terrible place, with danger on every side, he was suddenly and illogically seized with pity for his enemy. Valthor must be a very driven, lonely man. Perhaps even half-way to madness. Then Guyon shook his thoughts away and concentrated on Helmet memories, clear now. So long as there had been no major cave-ins, he knew exactly where to go.

"The side turning I spoke of is just a bit further down, now," he promised. "From the cave, we should be able to take a path down to the beach and work our way round. It'll be more exposed, but I don't trust these tunnels."

Jon nodded agreement. For the last few yards he had kept spinning round, sure he could hear something stealthily, menacingly following their trail. And though he had seen nothing, he wasn't convinced it was just imagination.

"Yes," he urged. "Let's get out! I think something's after us!"

Guyon frowned, but not with doubt.

"Right. As soon as we get to the side tunnel — which may be less well lit — you take the lead and help Zulie. You'll need to look out for potholes and I'll give Zulie my pole so she can probe the tunnel for any hanging obstructions. I'll guard our rear."

Without even thinking, he spoke to the boy as if Jon were his Athali, a trainee knight already, and Jon responded, straightening proudly and subduing his fears. Even though the light in the side tunnel was very dim, he barely hesitated before taking the lead. Zulie rested her left hand on his shoulder so he was free to use his crutches, and took the pole Guyon gave her. Already she could sense a new freshness in the air, a scent of the sea. But her other senses warned that Jon was right — something was following them. Something ferociously hungry.

"Take care, Guyon," she whispered, and the man smiled grimly, drawing his sword.

"Go on," he said "I'll keep just a little bit behind."

Quite still, he waited, scanning the walls, floor and ceiling of the tunnel entrance. A soft sound began as he watched, and with it the roof of the cave seemed to ripple slightly. Guyon leapt forwards and upward, his blade plunging into something that looked no different from the rocks over which it scuttled. Only when it fell to writhe obscenely at his feet, like a clockwork toy winding down, could he see that it was a centipede. An eyeless centipede, each leg as long as he was, and with a body at least four feet across and twelve feet long. Its mandibles looked capable of ripping a man apart and venom dripped from them as it died. Guyon shuddered and sent up a silent, heartfelt prayer of thanks to Yeveth. Then, after wiping his sword on the huge creature's body, he ran to rejoin his friends.

"Thanks for the warning, Jon," he said breathlessly. "I've dealt with our unwanted companion. Now let's get out fast in case it had friends. Do I see sunlight ahead?"

"Yes," Jon whispered. It was indeed sunlight, filtering in through the mouth of a cave, and he thought he had never seen anything more comforting and beautiful. When he spoke again the sound of his voice startled him by coming out deep, strong and full of confidence.

"Now, sir, Zulie, all we've got to do is find the ship!"

Guyon laughed, light-headed with relief as they moved into the sunshine.

"Yes," he exulted. "Valthor's trick has actually helped us to get ahead of him!"

Zulie's arm went round Jon's shoulders as they moved to the cave's mouth. Below them the sea moved peacefully, as unchanged by the world's tumult as Yeveth himself.

Then with one accord they moved to the mouth of the cave. There was no time to rest, not just yet. Maybe even now the Magos Lord was racing across the promontory above them.

Painfully, Valthor picked himself up from the debris of dust and stones, and the corpse of the haas beneath him. Its soft body had broken his fall, but he was still a mass of bruises, with a sharp pain in his chest that hinted of cracked ribs. Grimly he stared at his surroundings. Obviously, he had ridden over the fragile covering of greenery that concealed an old mine shaft and had fallen through it into one of the tunnels. There was no point in trying to climb to the surface again; the ship was close, and he could use this tunnel to reach it. If only he were not so terribly tired!

Even as a boy, Valthor had taught his body to endure, his will-power driving exhausted muscles to the limits of endurance, and then beyond. Once he had found triumph in the victory; but always, then, there had been a chance to rest. Now he dared not rest. The ship was close, but so perhaps were his enemies. He could sense their continued survival and it chilled him. How could any man escape certain death as often as Guyon did?

Allowing his body a few moments' respite, Valthor sent out mental probes, hungrily searching for an unshielded mind, trying to call his Magos allies to help him. But his mind too was drained, operating at only a fraction of its awesome power.

With a supreme effort, the Magos leader drew himself erect and began to move on. A shadow of fear touched him, but he would not let it remain, wouldn't acknowledge even to himself the possibility of defeat. Not now. He was Valthor — and even tired as he was, he had no equal, physical or mental.

The ship would be his. It was meant to be. It would be his right to lead his people into the power and glory of the Starborn, to break the feeble shackles of the past, of outdated Codes and Creed. One day people would look back and see his greatness, realizing at last that he had done what had to be done, what others had feared to do.

Ghosts flitted around him in this place of darkness where so many had died in slavery. Memories of people he had destroyed in his single-minded quest for power swarmed to accuse him, but Valthor dismissed them contemptuously. Such qualms of conscience were a luxury for the weak, for men who never realized that when a dream was great indeed, it justified any methods.

Grimly forcing himself to rise above agony and exhaustion, Valthor pressed on.

13

THE STARSHIP

It didn't take them long to climb down to the beach
— not by the path, for that turned out to be narrow
and dangerous, but by the rope of creepers taken
from the raft. Guyon anchored it to a rock in the
cave's mouth, then climbed down first to test it.
When it held firm, Jon and Zulie followed.

"We'll leave it dangling there," Guyon decided as
they moved off across the black sand.

"But how do we climb up once we get near the
ship?" Jon asked. "And what if the tide comes
creeping in?"

"It won't. Look."

Smiling, Guyon pointed to a line of white and
pink fragments of shell and coral, a definite stripe
on the dark volcanic sand.

"Bits swept off the reef to mark the limit of high
tide," he explained. "As for the ship . . . "

Suddenly his eyes looked beyond Jon, and into
Helmet memories.

"She lies waiting," he said almost dreamily, "in
the depths of an old crater. The whole crater has a
kind of movable roof, created by skills we can only
dream about. But there's another way in, through

a cave at beach level. It's concealed but I'll know it."

He paused, and his voice was full of yearning wonder when he spoke again.

"A ship from the stars!" he whispered. "Oh, just imagine soaring over our world and beyond — to worlds we can see now only as lights in the night skies."

"I dream of the healing knowledge she may hold," Zulie said, equally intensely. "I'm so tired of losing patients to death because I know so little! And . . . I want to live. Now more than ever!"

Jon didn't say anything; he just hurried down the beach, swinging along with practised ease on his makeshift crutches. Somehow he was more afraid than ever now that the ship was so close. Things were moving to a climax, but he felt like an actor in a play with the final scene still unwritten. Part of him trusted Yeveth. But Yeveth planned for the greater good, for the good of a whole world. And sometimes that seemed to mean that he had to allow bad things to happen to good people. Sir Kerouan was already dead. What if he had to die too, or Zulie, or Guyon, or all of them? Jon wanted desperately to run away, but he knew that if he did, he might never stop running — from himself, from life, from Yeveth. Whatever happened, Valthor must not get the ship!

Yet part of his mind argued, "You're still a boy. Handicapped, born in poverty, growing up a beggar. Why should you risk your life? You owe nothing to the world, to a god who's treated you so badly."

The thoughts settled like a dark cloud in the corners of his mind, and he slowed, aware that his twisted legs were aching fiercely, that he was hungry, thirsty and very tired. But then other pictures flooded into his brain: dreams and memories. Sir Kerouan lifting him out of the gutter; Zulie tending him lovingly; Almar with his slate and chalks and patience; Guyon . . . and that voice saying so very softly and gently, *You have more strength than you know. I will give you strength.*

"Yeveth," Jon breathed, and it was both a prayer and a promise. Even as he spoke the name he felt the dark cloud lift and new energy flow through him. Once again his crutches dug into the sand and he swung down the beach, followed by Guyon and Zulie. They jogged down the sand together, in tired and breathless silence, each lost in private thoughts.

"I want to live . . . "

Zulie heard her own words again and was startled by their hunger. She had convinced herself that she had accepted her disease, become resigned to its final phase coming to claim her life eventually. But she had been Sister Zulie then, working among the suffering poor. Now Lady Zuleika had reawoken, a bold, passionate woman with the blood of Knights Champion in her veins. A woman who remembered how to live and love.

What if the ship did hold healing secrets? Could she bear to yield them to the College of Healers, for careful testing and possible rejection of something that might save her own life? She had heard that in the past the Imperial Healers — who alone had the right to wear the Helmets — had refused some Starborn techniques as impossible or immoral. Would it be so very wrong to take the Helmets herself and check out their knowledge before passing them on to the College?

If, of course, she even dared to return. After Ill-arth, what if the knights truly believed she was a Magos, or blamed her for Sir Imar's death? So many people misunderstood and feared mind-link. They might kill her . . .

Guyon's arm was warm and strong under her hand. "I love him," Zulie thought, admitting it to herself at last. "For him, I want to live, as well as for myself."

Her perpetual darkness felt darker still as she fought with the anguish of her thoughts.

"Yeveth," she prayed silently, "I've been giving, serving, enduring for so long! Is it really wrong to take the chance of healing and happiness for myself before I pass it on to others?"

A stone, unnoticed by Guyon, caught under her foot and she stumbled, hating her blindness. Salt tears welled in her sightless eyes, but even as she wept she called silently, desperately to Yeveth. How could she think of possibly condemning other sick people to death in order to save her own life? Of course, any healing knowledge belonged with the College of Healers. As for being a Magos — she wasn't one, but she'd be as bad as any Magos if she took the Starborn secrets to protect herself.

As swiftly as it had come, the dark storm in her emotions passed over and she felt Yeveth touch her with his peace. Ashamed of herself, Zulie squeezed Guyon's arm for comfort and heard him whisper, "Not far now."

With the sun warm on her face, Zulie hurried on.

Guyon was not aware of the inner battles his friends had fought and won. His own battle had been short, sharp and swiftly over — just one more in a familiar series. True, he hadn't remembered the desolation of his punishment so vividly for a long time; the public humiliation as they stripped him of knighthood, placed the bar on his shield, and whipped him. Yet even as remembered pain seared him he also recalled the kindnesses: the messages from ordinary people he'd helped, saying he would always be a knight in their eyes; the way his stern adversary, Sir Andros, had smeared salve on his back after the beating. Things like that robbed the memories of their bitterness and swept away his temptation to use the ship for vengeance.

"From the dark side of myself," Guyon prayed as he ran, "Lord Yeveth, go on protecting me."

There would doubtless be more temptations. Guyon had never pretended to be a holy man, and he knew how much it would hurt to return, to face yet more Penitent Quests. It was not so much the danger that he feared but the knowledge that he would never dare speak of his love to Zulie. It wouldn't be fair while he remained a condemned man. But the alternative was unthinkable — to betray everyone's trust, and even Yeveth himself.

"But what if they do not use the ship for good?" part of him argued. "Kolris and Lorak mean well, but what of those knights who still think only of power and glory and conquest?"

"I'll fight that battle when I come to it!" Guyon snapped aloud to the voice within himself, then flushed with embarrassment as Jon skidded to a halt and turned, while Zulie gripped his arm anxiously.

"Sorry," he murmured. "Just arguing with myself. Being so near the ship and all it could mean is getting to me."

"Me too!" Jon exclaimed, relieved to share his fears. "I came over all scared and . . ."

" . . . and I wanted to take any healing secrets of the Starborn to save myself."

They stared at each other. Guyon said softly, "Could it be Valthor, Zulie? Breaking through our shields so cleverly that we become our own enemies? Or is it just — the seeds of evil in us?"

"Something more than both, I think," the Healer responded. She could sense the conflict flowing round them, something vastly more powerful than Valthor or themselves or any human being. Good versus evil. Yeveth versus the Evil One. They were part of the battle, and their souls part of the battle-ground. What could the ship hold that was so vital?

"Let's pray," she suggested. "Let's hold hands and ask Yeveth to protect us."

Gathered on the sand, with the sea roaring behind them, they reached out to each other and to the Lord they served. Eyes closed, they failed to see the huge creature which circled them briefly before winging its way to perch on the rim of the crater. It didn't matter anyway, for they were not the prey it sought. And when they opened their eyes, filled with new determination, it was gone.

The secret entrance to the cave of the ship was only yards away. It looked no different from the surrounding rock, but as Guyon, guided by the Helmet, pressed his fingers against the cliff face, ancient mechanisms moved into action and a door slid open. As it did so, lights blazed down the full length of a tunnel which stretched before them. Guyon stepped through first, his sword drawn, wary still of monstrous insects. But nothing moved, and the others followed him. Half eager, half afraid, they walked together down the corridor, Guyon slightly in the lead. He alone knew from the Helmet what he expected to find. Even so, he caught his breath as they rounded a slight bend in the tunnel. The reality was suddenly there in front of them, and they walked out of the tunnel into the crater itself.

Where the Starborn had placed a seal over the crater, nature had broken through, weakening the metal and tearing sections of it away. Now a living canopy of green vines and sweet-scented flowers hung high above them, and sunlight filtered through to fall in soft beams on the most beautiful sight Guyon or Jon had ever seen.

The ship had waited in lonely darkness for centuries, but she had been built to soar the skies and touch the velvet depths of space. Her silver hull curved with the grace of sculpture, and panels of something like crystallite glistened with jewelled radiance.

"She's lovely!" Guyon whispered. "Oh, Zulie — touch my mind and see her through my eyes!"

He could have offered no greater gift of love and trust. Tenderly, carefully, Zulie melded her mind with his and marvelled at the ship's beauty. Then all three of them moved forward together.

Guyon knew what he must look for: an engraved panel by a curving, wing-like projection. Finding it, he gently traced a pattern from his Starborn memories and waited. He heard nothing — no whirring or clanking of ancient machinery coming to life after a long sleep. Instead, a section of the hull slid open silently before him to reveal a small entrance chamber with an inner door.

"Let's go in!" Jon urged, but Guyon shook his head. In the first joy of seeing the ship he had almost forgotten Valthor — but not quite. Sword drawn, he quickly searched the crater and frowned at what he saw. If theirs had been the only entrance, except for the canopy above, it would have been easy to defend. But two other tunnels led into the crater, while a third had been only partly blocked by fallen stones. Valthor might even be in the ship already, like a spider waiting in its web.

"No," Guyon said quietly. "I want you to hide in some shadowed place where you can see those tunnels on the right, and the ship — but still be close enough to our tunnel for escape. I'll go in alone. Providing Valthor doesn't inconveniently turn up, I'll bring out anything I can carry for you to hide."

"Can't we just fly the ship out?" Jon suggested eagerly. "He'd never get us then. If the Helmet can tell you how . . . "

"It can, but no," Guyon said sadly, touching the projection near the door. It moved under his hand. Helmet knowledge came effortlessly into his mind and he spoke like a child reciting a familiar lesson.

"This is a vital control surface and rockfalls have damaged it. Any extra stress could tear it off and the ship would crash. It's better that you two escape with anything that can be carried, while I try to defend the ship against Valthor."

More than anything else, Jon longed to see inside this ship that had come from the stars. But he had grown up a lot and managed to swallow his yearning. Taking Zulie's arm, he guided her to a good hiding place in the shadow of the ship itself.

"I'll watch, Guyon," he agreed.

"And I'll give you silent warning if Valthor appears," Zulie promised. "But I dare not use my mind to try to locate him, for we'd betray our presence even as we discovered his."

Then she added, very softly, "Take care, Guyon."

"I will!" Smiling, the man turned and stepped into the ship, the inner door opening before him. As if some invisible being had reacted to his presence, all the lights in the ship blazed into life and he gazed in wonder at things no man now living had ever seen.

The first room he entered was, he guessed, the control room of the small ship. Dials, switches and screens waited patiently for knowledgeable hands to recall them to duty. Afraid to touch anything, Guyon walked carefully through and entered a corridor off which were eight further doors, one bearing a symbol which he knew from the Helmet was a warning not to enter. Leaving that door strictly alone, he opened one of the others and stared at totally unfamiliar machines, far too big to carry, grouped round a couch. In front of the couch, on a small table, were two Helmets. Guyon knew at once that this had been the ship's Sanctuary, a place of healing. Smiling, fear forgotten in hope for Zulie, he picked up the Helmets.

Then he continued his exploration. The next room appeared to be sleeping quarters, and yielded nothing. A third, larger room was quite empty. Guyon wondered if the Starborn had left behind them only a carefully selected legacy, devoid of anything which might do harm. So far he had seen nothing which could be a weapon.

A fourth room held more beds. On a small shelf next to one of them Guyon found a slender book bearing the symbol of the Way on its cover. Excitement grew in him as he flicked it open and gazed at strange yet familiar words, words much like the ancient high tongue used sometimes in ceremony by the knights and priests. Could this be the original Book of the Way, holding all the truth about Yeveth? He longed to try to read it, but knew there was no time. Returning to the entrance, he stepped back into the crater and ran over to where Jon and Zulie crouched in hiding.

"Treasures!" he said, his grey eyes radiant with joy as he handed the Helmets to Zulie and the book to Jon. "Healing Helmets and the legendary Book of the Way which our priests have wanted to find for centuries! Hide them safely on the beach somewhere. I'll stay in the doorway of the ship till you return, and keep watch for Valthor. Then I'll explore its other rooms."

"Healing Helmets!" Zulie whispered, all her dreams returning. But now her mind captured glorious visions of countless people for whom there had been no hope, who might now be restored to health by the new Starborn skills. In the surge of her delight she missed the dark, probing thought that flickered and was gone.

Eagerly, Jon led Zulie to the beach. Valthor was nowhere in sight and it was easy to hide the Helmets and the book under the sand. Jon marked the hiding place with an oddly-coloured stone, so he would be sure to find it again. Then they hurried back to the cavern. In their excitement, both forgot for a moment the threat of Valthor. Even Guyon, turning to smile at them as they came, took his eyes off the tunnel entrances.

Valthor, creeping silently towards the cavern from his side tunnel, took in the scene in one sweeping glance. A savage surge of joy filled him as he saw the Starborn craft, his passport to triumph, and his enemies off guard and at his mercy. He did not need to engage the powers of his mind. There were simpler ways. Without making a sound, he fitted an arrow to his bow. Then he rose like a menacing shadow from behind the stones that half blocked the tunnel. Guyon whirled, but Valthor's bow was already raised, his arrow aimed at Zulie.

"Yield the ship, Guyon," he said quietly, "or the Healer dies."

Jon gasped, and froze. For a second he thought of pushing Zulie clear, or shielding her with his own body, but he was terrified that he would be too slow. One mistake, and she would be dead. Zulie froze also, but not with fear. Slowly, proudly, she turned towards the sound of Valthor's voice.

"I'm not afraid to die," she challenged. "Guyon — don't yield to him for my sake!"

"Oh, but he will. He's always been a weak and gentle fool." The Magos lord laughed, and the bitter mockery in his laughter sent cold chills down Jon's spine.

"He ruined my first plans by protecting an old priest," the man continued. "But now he'll help me, to protect you. Boy, lead the Healer aboard the ship. You, Guyon, come out. Walk to your left, keeping well clear of them."

Jon hesitated, and the next command cut like a whiplash.

"Do as I say! Now! Don't you know I can take your mind and make you my helpless slave, boy?"

"Never!" Jon hissed. Guyon began to walk away from the ship.

"Do as he says, Jon," the Castelmaran murmured. "You too, Zulie. But you're making a big mistake, Valthor. This ship will crash if you try to fly it, and you can do nothing with it here."

"You lie."

"I'll show you the damaged part. Look, over here . . . "

Again Valthor laughed, this time even more terribly than before.

"You think I would fall for such a trick?" he mocked. Pausing, Jon half-turned to look at the Magos lord. Valthor's face was deathly pale, his eyes dark-shadowed and red-rimmed. He looked as if he hadn't slept properly for weeks. But the hand that guided the arrow was firm and, when he snarled another command, Jon flinched from the icy thrust of his mind.

"Into the ship, you two. Stand in the entrance. Guyon, throw down your weapons, and put your hands on your head."

At the entrance, Jon dared to look back over his shoulder. Guyon had obeyed Valthor's orders and was standing a few yards away, watching as Valthor emerged from his tunnel. The Magos lord's bow was still aimed and ready.

"So you have won, after all," Guyon said, desolation in his voice. His shoulders sagged and he looked so utterly defeated that Valthor paused, relaxing slightly as he enjoyed his triumph. It was enough.

Guyon moved like lightning. Leaping forward, he thrust Jon and Zulie into the ship's command room. Valthor's bow sang and Jon heard Guyon cry out as the arrow struck him, but he didn't fall. He whirled, reaching for the control that would shut the doors.

He almost made it.

Eyes blazing, Valthor leapt through the closing doors. He struck Guyon across the face, and this time the wounded man fell, choking back a groan.

"Guyon!" Zulie cried in anguish and started to crawl towards him. But Jon reached him first. The arrow had missed Guyon's body and gone through the upper part of his right arm. Its shaft had snapped as he fell and now he lay on his back, the point of the arrow protruding through his flesh.

Valthor didn't intervene as Zulie joined Jon. The Magos leader was staring round the starship's control room, smiling with deep satisfaction. Guyon's brief move had taken him by surprise, but now it no longer mattered. With the man wounded, he expected no trouble from the blind woman or the crippled boy.

The ship was his. And she would fly! A master of lies himself, Valthor didn't believe for one moment that Guyon had told the truth about the starship being damaged.

"With this ship," he exulted, "I will become Emperor of Rakath, then of the world. And then we will claim the stars!"

Guyon groaned softly as Zulie removed the arrow from his arm, but Jon's hand rested on his forehead and the boy's touch eased his pain. He didn't lose consciousness, but looked up at Valthor with no trace of despair in his grey eyes now.

"No," he said simply, "by now Sir Lorak will already have started rooting out your Magos followers. Even with Starborn knowledge and this ship, you can't hope to conquer the world. Everyone will stand against you."

For a moment, the Magos leader was silent. Then he said with chilling certainty: "It is my destiny to lead the Empire of Rakath into a brave new future."

Without warning, he invaded their minds, and

Jon shrank from his visions of city after city falling to this ruthless man with the light of madness in his eyes. Then the visions faded, and Valthor strode away from them to a major console. Now, as his mind yielded the Helmet's Starborn secrets, every knob, dial and indentation made sense. Smiling savagely, Valthor set a vertical take-off sequence in motion.

Jon didn't know what the Magos lord was doing. He only saw, in the man's concentration, a chance of attack or escape. Moving away from Guyon, he reached for his crutches. But the man called him back.

"No, Jon," he commanded softly. "He's too fast, too skilled. We can't stop him now. Only Yeveth can."

He would have said more, but the humming started. After her long sleep, the Starborn ship was awake and eager to reach for the skies again. The floor beneath them began to tremble as the hum rose into a song of power and the walls of the cavern started to move past the control room's viewscreens. They were flying!

"Crash couches," Guyon whispered, alerted by his own Helmet memories. Despite his pain, he felt strangely calm. They could do nothing to stop the take-off. But they could protect themselves — if Valthor would let them.

The starship shuddered violently as it tore through the tracery of green and into the open sky. A red light began to flash on the console in front of Valthor, then stopped.

"So you weren't lying," the Magos admitted. "One of the control surfaces is indeed damaged. But it'll get me to my stronghold. There, if you're not already dead from loss of blood, I will kill you, Guyon. In fact, I may throw you from the ship. But since the Healer — and, it seems, the boy — can mind-link, I shall study their minds before I destroy them."

"Oh, Valthor!" There was a note of anguish in Guyon's voice, deeper than physical pain.

"Why have you changed so much?" he asked. "Don't go through with this! Give yourself a second chance to be the man you were meant to be — an honourable knight!"

For a moment a look almost of regret flickered in Valthor's eyes. Then he shrugged and smiled, that proud, terrible smile.

"I have gone too far to turn back," he said fiercely. "One day history will record the greatness of my vision, and I'll have revenge for my years of exile."

His strong hands manipulated the controls, and the ship turned to fly over the sea.

"Help me to my feet," Guyon asked softly and, as Jon and Zulie obeyed, he turned to Valthor.

"There are crash couches here," he said, "set into the walls. Please let me lower two for Jon and Zulie, just in case."

Jon stiffened. He hated to see Guyon pleading with the evil Valthor. His own instinct was still to rush at the man. But Zulie held his arm and he sensed the warning in her mind.

No. Guyon is right. We can achieve nothing in our own strength. We must trust, Jon. Trust Yeveth. He will not let us down, even now, when everything seems lost.

Yet it was so hard to trust and do nothing! So hard to face Valthor's evident contempt.

"Why not?" the Magos agreed. "Those couches

173

have convenient straps. And since the boy would clearly love to attack me, it might be better to truss him up, and the Healer too. Do it, Guyon."

Silently the wounded man moved to the wall. He pressed two buttons, and parts of the metal were lowered to reveal great padded cushions made of some strange Starborn substance. As Zulie and Jon lay down on the couches, the cushions seemed to mould round their bodies, and straps emerged. Clumsily, handicapped by his injured arm, Guyon helped Jon and Zulie strap themselves in.

At an exclamation from Valthor, he turned. The Magos was staring at one of the screens.

"A sailing ship on the horizon," he mused. "The Emperor's questors, perhaps, arriving too late. I shouldn't let them go empty-handed."

As he spoke, he touched the controls again, and the ship slowed. A second movement set it hovering, under automatic control. Then Valthor rose from his seat, his sword in his hand.

"Your penitent quests are over," he said smiling, "but I shall be merciful, Guyon. I shall kill you cleanly before I send you plummeting down to the sea."

"You can try," Guyon responded, reaching for one of Jon's crutches. He had little doubt that he would be killed, but he would go down fighting.

"No!" Jon and Zulie screamed as one.

And then, like a deafening echo, the zaarl screamed.

Jon saw the creature first, its huge body filling the screen opposite him. The dragon-bird was enormous, perhaps twice the size of the one Valthor had ridden. Its skin was a deep scarlet, the colour of blood.

"A female," Guyon whispered, still poised to defend himself, "far from her mating grounds."

"They too can mind-link, over vast distances," Zulie said calmly. "They're the most intelligent creatures in the world, after us humans. You killed her mate, Valthor, and she has come for vengeance. She can sense your presence here."

The man hesitated, then moved back to the control panel. He knew that Zulie spoke the truth, for he sensed a mind-message of pure animal hatred. The zaarl was climbing, great wings clawing up the sky. It would swoop like a hawk on its prey. Valthor didn't think for a moment that its talons could pierce the hull of the Starborn ship, but Guyon's death could wait while he destroyed the zaarl. He punched a control which should have operated the ship's weapons, but nothing happened. He had no time even to wonder why before the zaarl struck, and the ship shuddered violently.

The zaarl did not understand the silver craft. It was far bigger than she, but hunger for vengeance overrode her natural caution. Though her talons could make no mark at first on this strange flying creature, she struck again and again, determined to tear through it and reach her prey within. The third time she struck, her talons gripped a projection from the silver creature, and she began to tear at it.

"Get us down, Valthor!" Guyon shouted. "It's got hold of the damaged control fin!"

The ship's wild lurch had thrown them close together. Guyon tried to reach the control console himself, but Valthor had no intention of yielding the controls or of landing the starship here, even to save his own life. On the screen he could see the sailing craft, close now, her shocked crew staring upwards. The imperial flag flew at her mast.

"No!" he spat. "Nobody shall take this ship but me, nor shall anyone take me alive!"

He thrust at Guyon, but a second lurch of the Starborn ship sent the Castelmaran tumbling backwards. Momentarily dazed, he lay where he had fallen.

Wriggling frantically, Jon managed to undo the straps which held him to his couch, and squirmed free of the cushions. It was difficult to move; he felt as if leaden weights had been fixed to his legs, while his head was drained and empty. But somehow he reached Guyon, and half-dragged, half-helped the hurt man to his own couch. There wasn't time to lower another one. The cushions of this couch would just have to protect them both.

"Thanks," Guyon whispered, as the control fin tore free. The ship's wild progress across the sky as Valthor fought to dislodge the zaarl ended abruptly. Now the silver craft spiralled downwards, sickeningly fast, as the sea rose up to meet them. Guyon was dimly aware of a soft whine, and knew that a Starborn safety mechanism had come into action, fighting gravity to break their fall. But surely it was too late.

The Starborn ship struck the sea in a hissing, tortured cloud of spray and her last bursts of power were silenced. Screaming in triumph, the zaarl wheeled away. She had avenged her mate, for she knew that within the broken silver creature the man she had tracked over land and sea lay broken too. Her fury gone, instincts older than anger claimed her. A queen of her kind, she must find a new mate. With slow and steady wingbeats, she began the long journey back to her mating territory.

In the unnatural stillness of disaster, Guyon was the first to move. His long years of penitent quests had taught him how to override pain and weakness. Calling on his reserves of strength, he freed himself from the couch and urged Jon to his feet.

"Help Zulie," he commanded breathlessly. "Get her to the door. The ship won't float for long."

Trembling, Jon obeyed. He could scarcely believe that they were still alive. But the crash couches had done their job and none of his bones seemed to be broken. Zulie was already undoing her straps.

Guyon made his way to the doors. The inner door was already open, but the outer one was still firmly shut. For a moment, Guyon paused, afraid to open it. He had no idea how low they lay in the water. The screens couldn't tell him, because they weren't true windows. They simply displayed what outside cameras recorded, and the cameras were wrecked. He only knew instinctively, by the feel of the ship, that she still floated but that they must get out fast.

As Jon and Zulie joined him, he took a chance and opened the doors. Mercifully, the mechanism still worked and, as the doors slid apart, water began to swirl in. But it wasn't a murderous flood.

"Praise Yeveth!" Guyon breathed. "We're safe now."

Some distance away the sailing ship, now anchored, was lowering men in a rowing boat. Guyon hailed them. Then he smiled at Jon and Zulie and urged them gently into the water.

"Swim towards that boat," he commanded. "I'll join you in a minute."

"But . . ."

"Come, Jon," Zulie said gently. She understood what Guyon had to do.

Valthor was sprawled on the floor of the control room, conscious but clearly in agony. Though he let no cry escape him, there was blood on his lips and more blood seeping through his clothing. His breathing came in tortured gasps. Jon, treading water, looked back to see Guyon kneel beside his enemy. Then the Castelmaran stood up and began to tow Valthor towards the door, using the increasing flood of sea-water to float Valthor's broken body.

Words from the Codes and Creed of Yeveth, which Jon had always thought rather stupid, echoed in his mind. "Love your enemy. Do good to those who hate you." Now Guyon was risking his life for his enemy, and it wasn't stupid at all. It was the bravest, finest thing Jon had ever seen.

"Guyon's trying to rescue Valthor. I must help him!" he cried to Zulie, but he'd barely managed three strokes when the starship tilted and slid silently beneath the surface of the sea.

"Guyon!" Jon screamed, striking out as fast as he could towards where the ship had gone down. Every stroke became an anguished prayer to Yeveth. Guyon mustn't die now, not when it was all over and they'd won. He mustn't!

"Yeveth!" Jon sobbed aloud, catching the echo of Zulie's own agony as she prayed. How long could a man hold his breath under water? It seemed as if Guyon had been under for ages. And he was wounded . . .

A wave slapped against Jon's face, choking him on salty water. But when it passed, he saw with almost unbearable joy that Guyon had surfaced.

Not only that, he was alive, turning on his back, floating.

"Thank you!" Jon whispered to Yeveth. Then he heard the creak of oars, and strong arms lifted him into the rowing boat. He recognized the crewman Zulie had saved when Sir Imar's ship was wrecked.

Then all he had endured in the past days came on him in a rush of exhaustion. He desperately wanted to see if Zulie was all right, and help the men get Guyon aboard. But the world wouldn't stay still. It swam round him in a dizzying grey whirlpool, dragging him down to its dark centre.

Just for a moment, Jon kept his eyes defiantly open. Then he lost consciousness.

14

NEW BEGINNINGS

Later, Jon could remember only the dreams. He had no recollection of days spent shivering or burning as the fever racked his body. He couldn't recall the long hours when Zulie, Guyon or some of the crewmen sat with him, giving him the drinks he called for in his delirium and bathing his burning skin. He did have a dim recollection of being taken on board a sailing ship, but after that there were only the dreams.

They weren't very pleasant — most of them were full of fighting. He dreamed of knights and warriors raiding secret Magos temples, demanding the cult followers' surrender. Healers who could mind-link were with the knights, shielding their minds from Magos attack, as well as treating anyone who was wounded. Sometimes the Magos fought back savagely; sometimes they surrendered, looking lost and afraid. And Jon saw in their eyes a reflection of Valthor, dying, his mind blazing a warning that the boy couldn't hear.

He saw a Rakathan vessel sail into Illarth, too, and Rakathan soldiers patrolling the streets where anyone who looked different had feared to walk. This dream was a good one, for he saw people daring to emerge into the sunlight, people with twisted bodies or minds that listened to a different song. Now at last they could be free and unafraid.

Sometimes voices drifted into his dreams, mainly Zulie's and Guyon's. After a while they seemed to get stronger, calling him back, until one day the dreaming ended and he opened his eyes.

To his amazement, he wasn't on a sailing ship, but in a Sanctuary bed. Zulie was bending over him, tears of joy in her eyes.

"Dear Jon!" she whispered. "Don't try to talk yet, you've been very ill. Just have a drink, and then we'll try you on some rich broth."

"What . . . ?" Jon started to ask, then gave in and drank as Zulie held a flask to his lips. It wasn't water, but aras juice. He drank gratefully, suddenly realizing how weak he was.

"You grazed your leg back in the mine tunnels," Zulie explained. "I don't suppose you even noticed it, but it gave entry to very nasty Starborn germs. Without the knowledge in the new Helmets . . . "

She shivered, and Jon didn't need to hear any more to realize he'd come close to death. Anxiously, he glanced down at his legs. Not only were they both still there, they were straighter! Zulie sensed his amazement and smiled.

"Yes," she said, "they're a lot better. I think the exercise you've had helped, and then during your fever you had violent spasms. When they passed, all your muscles relaxed and your legs straightened out."

For a moment Jon lay silent, getting used to the wonderful, impossible reality. Then he looked hard at Zulie. Surely she looked better too? Nothing could give her back her sight, but there was much more colour in her cheeks.

"Did the Helmets have a cure for lucar, too?" he asked very softly, and her answering smile was radiant.

"Yes! And for other diseases which we've been unable to cure before. Oh, Jon, you can't believe how marvellous it is for me, not having to fear any more, not having to wonder when the paralysis will start creeping over my body, or when my mind will begin to wander . . . "

Jon gasped. Zulie had always been so brave about her illness that he'd never grasped how awful it could be if it moved into the final stages. But now she was cured! With a deep sigh of relief, he fell asleep again. And this time, there were no dreams.

Over the next few days his waking periods grew longer, and he ate hungrily. Guyon came to see him and answered a flood of questions, first about the sailing ship that had come to their rescue.

"That crewman of Imar's who helped me find you in Illarth," the Castelmaran explained, "later rounded up some of his trusted mates. Together they commandeered a merchant vessel. They were going to sail it back to the capital, but then one crewman, who'd been Imar's steward, produced a scribbled chart. Apparently Imar had given it to him for safekeeping when the ship was wrecked. They decided to follow it — and arrived just in the nick of time to save us."

"And Valthor's dead?"

"He didn't want to live," Guyon said softly, almost sadly. "I tried to save him, but I was weak, and though he was badly hurt, he managed to break my grip. He died with his dreams.

May Yeveth have mercy on him — he tried to make amends."

"How?"

"Lorak organized raids on the Magos strongholds Valthor had established. But his men reported that many of the cult members surrendered freely. They said Valthor had sent them a last mind-message warning that he had been wrong, and that they couldn't fight the living power of Yeveth."

Jon remembered his dreams, and wondered if they had been dreams, after all. He would have to ask Zulie to teach him how to handle those fragments of other people's thoughts that he kept picking up accidentally. But he said nothing of this to Guyon. Instead he asked, "What about the Starborn ship?"

"It's still lying in twenty fathoms of water. We lack the skill to raise it."

Guyon paused thoughtfully, then shrugged.

"Priest Parl thinks Yeveth meant it to end this way," he said. "He thinks we're not yet ready for the power that starship could give us. He also believes we found everything that Yeveth really wanted us to have — the Healing Helmets and, above all, the Book of the Way."

"Have you read it?" Jon asked. Guyon shook his head.

"The priests and scholars are translating it now," he explained. "I managed to understand only a bit of it when I tried to read it on the voyage back. I speak the high tongue of knights, not scholars, and there's a difference. But . . . "

His grey eyes lightened with excitement and he smiled, moving closer to the bed and dropping his voice to a whisper.

"But from what I could understand, Jon, it's powerful stuff! Over the centuries I think many of the nobles, and some of the priests, have rewritten the Way to suit their own ends. They tried to turn Yeveth into a fierce and proud warrior God, who favoured the aristocracy! But this Way is all about love, justice and mercy. It's about Yeveth's love for the despised and powerless, not just the great and the good. It's a Way that allows even the most wicked person to be changed by Yeveth's love. It could turn our whole world upside-down!"

Jon grinned at Guyon's enthusiasm, but he looked a bit uncertain. "I hope it doesn't, yet," he muttered. "I think I've had enough excitement for a while!"

"You've also done enough talking for a while," Zulie scolded gently from the door of the room. "I want you to eat something now, Jon, then sleep. When you wake, we'll do some gentle exercises. And you, Guyon, have a visitor."

Her whole face blazed with love as she turned to smile at the man, and Jon grinned again. So that was the way the wind blew! Well, he wasn't surprised and he rather liked it. His childhood as a beggar in the slums, with a prostitute for a mother and a drunk for a father, hadn't given him a high opinion of romantic love. But with these two he suspected it would be very different. Guyon's face was reflecting all the radiance in Zulie's, and he looked at her as if she was the loveliest woman in the world.

Jon asked innocently, "When are you two getting married?" and they both blushed like teenagers. Then Guyon laughed.

"You'll be the first to know," he promised. "We'll

have you as an attendant, all dressed up in an embroidered suit and carrying Zulie's posy."

"Oh, no you won't!" Jon protested, then joined in Zulie's laughter. Because of course Guyon wouldn't mean a horrible threat like that — would he?

"You'd best not keep Sir Lorak waiting," Zulie reminded Guyon, and the man raised his eyebrows.

"Lorak? Where is he?"

"Upstairs, in Almar's study."

"I'll go to him now."

"And I'll bring you something to eat, Jon."

It was only after they'd both gone out of the door that Jon realized he hadn't asked one vital question. Was Guyon still condemned to his penitent quests? He decided to ask Zulie when she returned. But meanwhile, because he still tired more easily than he wanted to admit, he settled back in bed and closed his eyes. Soon voices began to drift down to him, from the open window of the study above. Lorak did most of the speaking.

"Parl says the translation is almost finished," Lorak said, "and he already fears its teachings will be rejected by some of the old aristocratic families — yes, and some of the priests. They're already angry over some of the reforms Emperor Kolris has made recently. And he's sure to make more if he chooses to live by the Way."

"Which he will," Guyon murmured. "He is a very good and extremely determined young man."

"There could be plots, rebellion and division. The Empire will need a very special Knight Champion."

"Yes. It will be hard to find someone to replace a knight as brave, honourable and good as Sir Kerouan was."

Both men fell silent for a moment; then Guyon

said clearly, "It's a pity we can't wait about twenty years. I have a feeling that lad Jon will grow into a fine knight, or Healer, or both."

Jon sat bolt upright in bed, his eyes and mouth wide open. Had Guyon really said that about him? A warm glow of delight rushed through him, followed by the oddest feeling of humility. He wasn't really that special. Guyon couldn't know how he'd once been a thief and a liar as well as a beggar, and how in the past weeks he'd spent at least half his time really scared. It was only Guyon himself, and Zulie, and . . . yes, and Yeveth, who had helped him to come through.

But . . . "a fine knight or a Healer or both . . . "

"Oh, Yeveth!" he breathed. "If only I could! Will you help me?"

The men must have moved away from the window, for he heard no more of their conversation. And when Zulie came in with a bowl of stew, he settled down obediently to eat. Then he slept, with real dreams this time, joyful and thrilling dreams of the futures that might be his.

Knight, or Healer, or both — Yeveth would surely guide him when the time came.

Zulie came in once more, to touch his sleeping body and make sure that all was well. Then, with joy in her heart, she went to join Almar at his evening clinic. Thanks to the Helmets, they could cure so many more people now!

Guyon, bidding farewell to Sir Lorak, watched her go and forced himself not to call out after her. He also looked in on Jon, but left the boy sleeping. Then he wandered down to the waterfront. There, Apprentice Cella was handing out free bowls of food to local street children and Guyon, lost in thought, was startled to find one of them suddenly standing before him. The boy didn't look up — perhaps because one eye was nicely blackened from a fight — and he shuffled his feet. But he said gruffly, "I'm Bok, mister. You saved my life and I never said thank you."

Guyon smiled.

"My pleasure," he murmured. "Dare I ask if you've given up a life of crime?"

"Sort of," the boy muttered. It hurt his pride to admit that he and his friend Freth had now decided they weren't that good at stealing, and were giving the Brown Brothers and their school another try.

"Jon . . . he did all right, didn't he? Is he going to get better?"

"He is," Guyon promised.

Then Cella called "Seconds!" and Bok looked pleadingly at Guyon. The knight smiled.

"I'll tell Jon you were asking about him," he promised. "Now go and get your extra helping. I imagine you could do with it!"

But as the boy hurried away to join the queue of children, Guyon stood quietly, lost in thought. With hands that trembled slightly, he reached for the pendant Lorak had given him, and traced the symbol of the Way. Not a broken sword after all, but something on which Yeveth had died, giving his life to defeat evil and then returning to life to defeat death. The Eternal One, indeed, who somehow managed to be God, and man, and above all, an ever present friend.

"I need you now, Lord, more than ever," Guyon said softly, thinking of the last and most demanding penitent quest that had been laid upon him; to take Sir Kerouan's place as Knight Champion of the Rakathan Empire. He had never felt so inadequate to any task in his life. Then he rose and went back to the Sanctuary.

The quest was over. The Way was beginning.

SHAPE-SHIFTER:
THE NAMING OF PANGUR BÁN
The first in the Pangur Bán series

Fay Sampson

Deep in a dark cave in the Black Mountain, a
witch was plotting mischief: 'We need
something small, something sly, to carry a
spell . . . and then we shall see who reigns on
the Black Mountain!'

Shape-Shifter, the kitten, is her victim.
But, before the charm is complete, he
escapes. He finds himself caught in a spell
that has gone wrong and a body that is not
his own.

In blind panic, he brings disaster even to
those who want to help him. Only a greater
power can break the spell.

ISBN 0 7459 1347 4

OPERATION TITAN

Dilwyn Horvat

'Far out beyond the orbit of the planet
Saturn, space stretched endlessly, cold, dark
and silent. Into the emptiness the mighty
flagship *Conqueror* emerged, its wedge-
shaped bulk slicing into the space-time
continuum.

   'Other craft appeared until finally a total of
twelve warships powered in towards the
speck that was Titan.'

   The Empire rules by fear. It destroys all
who oppose it. For the rebels on Titan escape
seems impossible. In a desperate race against
time, Paul Trentam sets out from Earth on a
perilous rescue mission . . .

ISBN 0 85648 501 2

ASSAULT ON OMEGA 4

Dilwyn Horvat

'The planet lay like a diamond on the velvet of space. Mark and Paul watched in silence as their craft drew away from it, the hidden fortress, a refuge for those whom the Empire was determined to destroy.

'Ahead was the quest for a woman called Natasha, and a confrontation with the age-old enemy, the wielder of darkness.'

This gripping sequel to *Operation Titan* tells of a daring rescue bid — on the Empire's most notorious prison-camp, *Omega Four*.

ISBN 0 7459 1048 3